ARC

Love on the Prairie

Ciara Knight

LOVE ON THE PRARIE

Book I
McKinnie Mail Order Bride Series

First edition published 2017

Cover art ©2017 by Yocla Cover Designs
Edited by Cora Artz
Copy Edit by E. Sewell.
Interior Design: Airicka Phoenix
Formatter: Airicka Phoenix

ISBN: 9781939081643
Published by Ciara Knight
Also available in eBook and paperback publication.

Love
on the
Prairie

Prologue

Abigail McKinnie and her six sisters huddled together for the last time. Ashes and debris littered the floor of their half-demolished home, the smell of burned wood, gunpowder, and Yankee stench still haunting the air.

Everything was gone. Not just their possessions, but their dreams, too. All lost to the wake of the Yankees' pillaging.

Cora, her closest sister in age and friendship, curled into Abigail's side, resting her hand on the waist of her dress. "I know it isn't the latest fashion, but I did my best."

Abigail fluffed the limp skirt which had once billowed out over a grand hoop. She squeezed her sister against her side. "Not your fault those Yanks pillaged our home." She sighed. "It'll do."

Laughter from two of her sisters sang through the room where they had all slept since that horrible night. The once-grand parlor had been reduced to tatters, the walls smeared with soot. Surrounded by destruction, it warmed Abigail's heart to hear some sign of happiness in their world. "Going to take a walk," Dinah announced.

"Be home before sundown." Abigail ordered, knowing dangers still lurked around the plantation.

Dinah nodded and took Josephine by the hand, the rest of her sisters except Cora followed them around the half-burned wall and onto the front porch, disappearing from Abigail's sight.

Cora stood and eyed the length of the skirt. "It should be suitable for travel, but perhaps I should hem it a little higher. I wouldn't want you tripping and twisting an ankle."

Abigail's heart ached at the thought of leaving her, of leaving all her dear sisters. "We won't be separated for long."

Cora just smiled and took both her hands, squeezing them tight. "Promise me you'll try to make this work. Our cousin is a good man and you'll be safe there, and have a home again."

"A home? I admit I'm glad to be leaving this haunting ruin, but home for me is to be with my sisters. This is a cruel punishment, crueler than anything Sherman and his men did to us." Abigail studied the faded lace on the bodice of her once-elegant gown. Now old, stained, and out of fashion, it was one of the few things she had left besides her sisters. "Listen, try to stay a little longer. Don't accept a mail-order proposal yet. I know you all need to leave this place, but I've spoken to the Whitakers and their son will bring food as he can. I know I can convince Mr. O'Brien to bring all of you to his homestead so we can be together."

Cora sighed. "I knew it was strange that you agreed to this so quickly. My dear sister, the same one who swore she would never marry after William died."

A jolt of grief twisted her heart, making it ache more than the wave of terror and destruction the Yankee army had brought to their plantation.

Cora stroked her cheek with the kind of love only a sister could offer. "You know we can't stay here. Our lands are scorched. Our house is destroyed." Her voice lowered. "Our souls have suffered. Josephine is ruined, and nightmares still plague her from…from the attack," she managed, her voice cracking with grief.

Abigail squeezed Cora's hands tighter, refusing to allow herself to be consumed by the past. "I know, and I'm not asking you to try to rebuild. I think it's time to let go of our heritage, of our father's house. There is nothing left for us here. Our slaves have abandoned us, our lands are dead, charred, torn up, and unfarmable, our house is but two rooms that remain standing. If only we had fertile land, supplies, farm equipment, animals, anything, I'd stay and make this work. We would make it work."

Cora nodded but didn't say a word. She only stood with the look of loss in her gaze. Abigail swallowed her regrets of not being able to protect her sisters better. "We have found nothing but loss in this place. Our father, mother, and brothers are all gone. Our great grandparents braved the oceans to settle here; I can brave a train ride. I will succeed in convincing Mr. O'Brien to keep us together. I fear if you leave I may never find you again." Her voice cracked, but she cleared her throat and continued, knowing she couldn't lose her sisters, too.

"Please, just promise me you'll hold off on the mail-order bride agreements. Even just a week or two." She leaned her cheek into Cora's hand. "I cannot imagine never seeing you again, or feeling your touch on my cheek, hearing your words, laughing with you." That familiar lump rose in her throat, but it didn't carry with it tears as it usually did. She'd learned a long time ago that tears were nothing but a waste of valuable energy.

Cora lowered her hand to her side. "I will do what I can. If anyone can convince a man to provide for a woman and all of her sisters without marriage being involved, it's you. After all, you convinced our father to buy us all dresses when we already had too many to fit in our rooms. You convinced that merchant to give us credit even after our slaves abandoned the fields. You even convinced the town to help in the fields to save our lands, if only for a time. You, my dear sister, can convince anyone of anything." Cora smiled, a sweet knowing smile only she possessed.

"I hope you're right. The thought of us being split up, spread throughout the wilds of the west, frightens me. The thought of you married off to some stranger and being forced to live in the rugged Rocky Mountains, or Dinah ending up in the Plains, and Elizabeth—"

"Stop, please. I cannot bear to think of it." Cora stepped back. "I promise we'll wait as long as we can, but we're running out of options. Go. Try and convince Mr. O'Brien that his family needs him, and send me word as soon as you can."

"I don't see how he could refuse us," Abigail said with a confidence she didn't feel. "We might be women, but we are strong. We can cook, clean, work the fields, whatever he needs."

Cora nodded. "Just promise me one thing."

"What's that?" Warning prickled along Abigail's skin and she knew she didn't want to hear her sister's next words.

"If you can't convince him to take all of us in the beginning, at least convince him to take Josephine first. After all she's been through, she needs a safe place where she is surrounded by people she can trust. Then work on convincing him to take the next youngest and on up the list. I, my dear sister, am last."

She shouldn't have been surprised. Cora was always sacrificing herself for the sake of others. Yet, Abigail could only gape at her for a moment. "What? No, I—"

"Think about it, Abby. Apart from you, I'm the eldest. Some would consider us spinsters." Cora dropped her gaze to the dress in Abigail's hands, the one she'd once worn to meet her fiancé before he left for war. "If we hadn't been promised…if the war never happened, our lives would be different. It's the same for many others in town. With all of our men gone, we have no prospects here in the South, and I refuse to marry a Yankee. Not after…" Her voice faded, no doubt getting lost amongst the memories of the horrors of war. Despite putting on a brave face, Abigail knew Cora had suffered more than most. After witnessing her fiancé's and brother's murders at the hands of a Yankee soldier, she had every right to harbor hatred.

Cora stood, her McKinnie Irish red hair cascading down her back. She eyed Abigail's carpetbag. "Brother's clothing? I don't see why…" She sighed and shook her head. "Never mind. I would try to convince you to marry him, settle down, and make a new life, but I know you will not be persuaded. I knew you had other plans when you agreed to go instead of sending Josephine. Will you at least promise me to keep an open mind? Our cousin is a fair, gentle man. You could do much worse."

"He *was* gentle, and awkward, and quiet, but men change." Abigail couldn't help but compare him to William, the man she'd chosen to marry. The man she would have married had war never broken out. It seemed like four lifetimes ago now, back when the lands and people were unchanged and familiar.

"If anyone can persuade him, you can." Without another word, Cora glided into the other room to join the rest of their sisters outside. Abigail could hear their muted conversation, somber compared to the laughter that had once filled these rooms. Abigail closed her carpetbag then gazed through the cracked window at their once glorious, green plantation. Now scorched, the landscape seemed to be dying a slow death, just like their happiness. They needed to move forward. They needed to leave this place before they all starved. It broke her heart to let go of the land her grandparents had settled, the home her father had built, but right now survival mattered more.

After months of searching for a way to save her sisters from destitution, this plan seemed to be the only option. Although she would've preferred to starve than marry any man other than William, she'd learned a long time ago that she could only rely on herself and her sisters. Giving a man control over her life would prove to be disastrous when all they seemed capable of was abandoning, pillaging, and dying.

Owen Baker patted the dirt then straightened to look down at the new grave. O'Brien. His farming partner, his friend, his savior. The man who took Owen in after his bride and her son died. His third burial since arriving in Kansas. As breathtaking as the prairie was, it was definitely no place for weak men, women, or children.

His only neighbors, Martin and Susan Dunst stood by his side to pay their respects. A short ceremony, with no words and no tears, but full of sadness.

"Willy O'Brien was a good man, for an Irishman," Martin said, his tone somber instead of his usual teasing. Being German, Martin would always flip Willy playful insults about his homeland, but the Irishman gave as good as he got.

Their colorful bantering had added entertainment to Owen's mundane prairie life.

Susan gripped Martin's forearm and held him tight. "It's unfortunate, but it was O'Brien's time to go home to our Lord." She let go of her husband then nodded to Owen. "I'll go wait by the wagon while you two say your goodbyes." She slipped away, but not before kissing two of her fingers and pressing them to the top of the cross marking Emma's grave, then doing the same for her son. Owen swallowed. He'd only been a father for a week to the five-year-old, but the sight of the cross still pierced his heart. The child had been robbed of life too young.

With a pause, Susan glanced over her shoulder at him. "We'll stop in from time to time, but our home is always open to you."

Owen placed his hat on his head and offered a simple smile. If he'd learned anything out on the prairie, it was that neighbors, even though they were few and far away, were often all a man had. Martin shook Owen's hand and nodded his agreement. "I'm not much for goodbyes, so I'm going to head out with Susan, but I'll be back around soon. Make sure you don't stay out here alone for too long. Perhaps you could go into

Prairie City more often. Or maybe you could get yourself one of those mail-order brides. We don't want you suffering from Prairie Madness."

While Owen had never witnessed a case of Prairie Madness, it didn't surprise him that men could go mad from the solitude out here. "Not gonna bring another person out here to die, especially a fragile woman. Until I get a house built and settle this land, I don't want to subject a woman to this life."

Martin placed his hat on his head. "My Sue has done well." He smiled, that friendly, down-home kind of grin. "You need to order yourself a tough German girl."

The prairie wind stirred the tall brown grass as if agreeing with the older man, but Owen ignored them both. He didn't want another mouth to feed, or to have to take care of someone when they caught a fever or had an accident. He looked down at the three graves. Or to worry about them just up and dying on him. "I don't think I could handle a German woman. She might be too tough for me."

Martin laughed from the gut, loud and deep. "You might be right." They walked to the wagon, and Martin climbed up on the buckboard next to Susan. Martin gave a nod in farewell and then clicked the reins. A few minutes later, the sound of the horses' hooves thumping against the ground and the squeak of the wagon's wheels faded in the distance, leaving Owen alone. Again.

He removed his hat and wiped the sweat from his brow on the sleeve of his shirt. A dip in the creek would feel good about now, but he needed to tend to Willy's affairs first. He was hoping he'd find a letter amongst Willy's things, something with information on where he could send Willy's few possessions. His friend hadn't been married, but he had occasionally mentioned something about bringing a girl out to the prairie. Owen had advised his friend against that plan. He glanced at the cross marking Emma's grave. The prairie was unkind to even the most hardened of men.

Owen planted his hat back on his head, grabbed his shovel, and headed for his dugout. Simple, comfortable, and quiet, the earthen structure was the perfect temporary home until he could get a real house built. He'd hoped to have Willy's help with that, but now the task fell solely to him.

A gentle breeze drifted past, carrying with it the scent of damp earth. A sure sign there'd be rainfall that night, Owen smiled. *Good,* he thought. Rain would soften the earth for planting. Even though he hadn't made it all the way to California like he'd planned, he could still make it work here. He stepped over the rocks and walked along the creek bed until he reached the front door of the dugout. Willy had graciously let Owen stay in his home while he built his own, but now he guessed he didn't need to rush to build his home on his own land. It would be awhile before any other homesteaders would want to claim the property, and it was on the edge between he and Willy's land.

He settled his hat on the hook by the door then knelt beside Willy's bed to pull out the box of possessions Willy had kept underneath. At least he'd get to sleep in a real bed tonight instead of a pile of hay on the ground. Guilt tickled the back of his neck at the thought of carrying about the man's bed when he'd just buried him. Even if the Irishman had been too weak, too gentle, too soft to survive out here, he had been kind.

With a sigh, Owen yanked the small box out, sending a puff of dust and dirt into the air. He didn't like digging through someone else's things, but what choice did he have?

Willy had mumbled his last wishes about a bride, but Willy had never married. Of course, he'd been mad with fever after his fall. Infection and pain his mind before the Lord took his body.

He opened the box and found a stack of letters written in perfect penmanship. A lady's handwriting, no doubt. *Probably Willy's mother*, Owen thought. Thank goodness Willy hadn't gotten married. What would Owen have done with a helpless female out here? He'd already abandoned his plan to journey out west, settling here when his new bride became ill. Yet despite them remaining behind, she had succumbed to the illness fast.

He shook off the dark memories and eyed the return address. It was from a town in Georgia called Marietta. He slid the letter from its envelope and read the message.

Mr. O'Brien,

I write to you in regards to the marriage agreement you had proposed several years ago. I am now ready to accept. While my father is now gone, I know he would be pleased with this decision. Please write and inform me of your answer.

Sincerely,

Abigail McKinnie

Owen grabbed the next letter, hoping it would be about Willy's refusal, but with the first line his worst fears came true.

Mr. O'Brien,

Thank you for your expedient reply. I need to settle my family's affairs, but I will leave for Prairie City, Kansas two days hence. I look forward to our reunion.

Sincerely,

Abigail McKinnie

He flipped the page over, but it was blank. Then he spotted the date scribbled in the top left-hand corner. *July 15, 1865*. Her only options were to travel by train or wagon or coach, and rail seemed the more likely choice for an unmarried woman. But that meant she'd be here any day now. Even if he wrote to warn her not to come, the letter would arrive long after she had left Georgia.

Wait, were the railways even running right now? He remembered reading in the newspaper about Sherman's march devastating the Southern states while in town months ago. He rifled through the rest of Willy's legal papers and a family photo of elegantly-dressed women, which only caused his fear to grow. No woman could survive on this land.

Not with Indians, disease, hard labor, and isolation. Especially not some Southern belle. She'd die for sure. And she'd arrive to no husband, or man to care for her. What would happen to her when she stepped off the stage coach and there was no one to collect her? Even if he wanted to, it would be too late. The woman could've arrived yesterday.

He headed outside for some fresh air, to think and figure out what to do, but didn't find answers. Nothing but rolling hills, tall grass, and the occasional clump of trees for as far as he could see. It was a land worth settling.

As he watched the sun reach the peak of midday, a red dot came into view over a hill, It grew larger, into more of a figure as it steadily approached. A woman's figure, no doubt about it with that fancy dress and delicate frame. Well, at least this saved him from having to try to track her down in Prairie City. He squared his shoulders and marched to meet her before she could even step foot on his land. With a determined attitude, he stopped a few feet from her before she even looked up to notice him.

Startled, she stopped in her tracks. She was a beauty, he'd give her that, even despite being worn out, flushed, obviously tired.

He needed to send her home immediately, before she fainted from exhaustion or fell ill. He'd hitch the team and drive her into Prairie City for the night. Before she could open her mouth, he announced, "O'Brien is dead. Go home."

He expected shock or grief, but she only stared at him for a moment. Then her head angled to the side and she took a long, exaggerated breath. "Is that any way to tell a lady her intended has passed?"

Stunned, he shook his head slowly, his mouth opening, but nothing came out. Was she really so unconcerned?

"Fine, he's dead. Is this his land?"

Owen looked behind him at the dugout, tiny barn, even smaller shed, and fencing that stretched for miles to either side of the small homestead then back at her and nodded. "Yeah, but—"

"He was family. It's mine now."

Chapter Two

Abigail stumbled down the hill, both her feet flaming lumps of pain. Wearing ankle boots in this terrain had been a bad idea, but they were the only shoes she owned. Her back wailed with the need to sit down and rest, but she refused to let that man see her collapse from exhaustion. No, she'd make it to the home her cousin had built under her own steam and then fall into any bed it offered. Tomorrow she'd deal with this new mess she'd found herself in.

The man blocked her path, his hands in the air as if to stop her. "You don't understand."

She didn't respond. As far as she was concerned he was a stranger, a stranger who in her blurry-eyed state looked like the most handsome man who ever breathed, despite his torn, dirty clothes and scruff-covered face. Convinced delirium had taken hold, she shook her head in an attempt to clear it, but the handsome stranger remained in her path.

“Ma’am, wait. You can’t stay here.” The man’s voice sounded urgent, but still she ignored him. With the small earthen structure the only thing in her sight, she stumbled toward it.

The blisters from her shoes stung her toes like thousands of fire ants, and she quickened her pace, desperate to sit down and free her feet. In her haste, she tripped over the hem of her skirts for the thousandth and one time since she had started her journey.

The man leapt to her side, but she slid away, hiked up her skirts, and continued forward. Now wasn’t the time for decorum. She needed to bathe and sleep. At this point, bathing was optional despite the days worth of filth and the unladylike aroma she was sure overpowered her perfume after over two weeks of traveling.

“How’d you get here?” He shuffled ahead of her and took his hat off before blocking the door to the odd-looking structure built into the side of a hill. The land didn’t look anything like Georgia. With nothing but open fields of tall brown grass, it felt barren and empty.

"Walked," she mumbled, her eyes on the chair she spotted just beyond the crude curtain flittering in the wind that served as a makeshift door. Could this even be classified as a dwelling? She'd thought traveling by train and coach was rough, what with the constant bouncing, odd conversations, and smell she had endured between St. Joseph and Kansas City. Yet, a few miles into her walking journey and she would've given anything to return to that cushioned seat.

"From Prairie City?"

"No. From Gardner." Abigail fought the sway in her body and gripped the side of the wood and grass structure.

"Gardner… That's almost twenty miles."

"I'm aware of that. If you don't mind, sir, I'd like to sit down. And some water, then we can speak." She thought about shoving him from the doorway, but she didn't possess the strength. She barely had the energy to remain standing.

"I'll fetch water, you sit. I'll take you to Prairie City before the sun goes down and you can stay in town. I'll pay for the inn and the train fare back to where you came from." He side-stepped and offered her entry into the strange structure.

She took a step forward and a mouse skittered over the dirt floor, up the wall and into the grass roof overhead. She didn't care. Despite her blistered feet, exhaustion, and the shock of hearing about her cousin, she still refused to let a man take care of her. Dropping her carpetbag on the floor, she snatched a bucket hanging from a nail by the door then turned and headed toward the well.

"Ma'am, you need to sit down before you collapse. You're going to make yourself sick." He chased after her with pleading eyes and grabbed for the bucket, but she yanked it away.

"I'm fine," she said with as much grit as she could muster. Yet, her head screamed at the aches and pains riddling her body. She refused to show weakness. She couldn't, not if she was going to fight to keep her cousin's land and make a home for her sisters out of this barren place. Barren but hopefully fertile.

She reached the well and turned the handle to bring up the bucket, but her arms were weak from fatigue and hunger. With each turn, she only managed to bring the bucket up a few feet before her hand would slip and the bucket would fall back down to the bottom again. Using every ounce of strength she had left, she yanked on the handle once more but fell against the well.

The man grabbed her around the waist to keep her upright, but she shoved him away. Before she could utter a protest, he picked her up and sat her to the side. “Enough,” he said in an authoritative tone. He cranked the handle with little effort, poured water into the bucket and then hauled it to the house.

Weakly, she followed. By the time she reached the doorway he had a tin cup of cool water waiting for her at the table.

“Sit. Drink,” he ordered.

Abigail shuffled to the chair and collapsed onto the hard wooden seat. It wasn’t one of her mother’s plush settees, yet she’d never been so happy to sit down in all her life. When Confederate army had taken over their home, they had even stripped the fabric from the furniture.

Abandoning decorum once more, she gulped down the water in a matter of seconds. Liquid dripped down her chin and she swiped it away with the back of her hand. She eyed the seedlings resting in the corner, waiting to be planted. There was life here.

He shook his head and retrieved the bucket to refill her cup. "Name's Owen Baker."

"Abigail McKinnie. What happened to Mr. O'Brien?" She lifted her right foot and unlaced the boot. Then she froze, only now realizing she was alone with a man who could be an outlaw.

He chuckled and leaned against the side of the table, crossing one foot over the other. His broad chest stretched the front of his shirt and the buttons threatened to pop off in protest. "I didn't kill him if that's what you're thinking. He died of fever, like most others 'round these parts. Buried him a few hours ago. This place isn't for the weak…or ladies such as yourself. That's why you have to go back home. You have no idea how rough life is out here on the prairie. I can't be watchin' out for you on top of doing what needs to be done to get this place running."

She straightened. "I can take care of myself. And I'll worry about how to run my land. Were you Mr. O'Brien's steward or something?"

Owen shoved from the table and paced the floor. "No. Willy and I were working together. We managed to secure most of what we need to start breaking the land and prep it for planting next season. I'd promised to help him with his land and we shared this home while we were working together. Once both crops were planted, I'd build my own home."

Gingerly, she slid the boot from her left foot, biting her lip to keep from screaming. Blood stained her stockings and she knew it would be difficult to walk tomorrow, let alone work, but she'd manage. She always managed.

She removed the left shoe with the same delicate movements, but her skin protested. The dried blood had cemented her heel to the leather. After a moment, she worked it free and dropped the shoe to the floor. Her stockings were ruined, the only dress she had left was ruined, her feet were ruined, and now her plan to save her sisters was ruined.

With a glance around the small space, she scrutinized the simple amenities. Dirt floor, wood stove, a straw pile in one corner, and a bed in the other. Simple, but it was more than she'd had for the last week. Seeing a sheet of paper on the floor near the bed, she recognized her handwriting and realized it was one of the letters she'd written to her cousin. Did he know why she was here? Was that why he was so insistent she go back home, because he was trying to steal her claim? A claim that would allow her and her sisters to start over. When their brothers had gone to war and her little brother and parents had died, managing the plantation had fallen to her and her sisters. They had to work the fields after their slaves had fled, but now the land was too scorched to grow anything.

“I know how to plow and plant. I’ll manage,” she said, her voice cracking from exhaustion.

Owen ran a hand through his hair and shook his head. “You don’t understand. This is man’s work. This ground is hard, not like what you’re used to in Georgia.” He faced her with a determined expression then his gaze slipped to her bloodied feet. “Dear God. What happened?”

She slid her feet back under her skirts. “Nothing. I’m fine.”

He dropped to his knees in front of her and glanced up with a look of terror, as if she’d just brought the cholera epidemic to his doorstep. “Don’t be stubborn. Let me see,” he said in a softer, concerned tone.

Abigail didn’t know if it was his pained expression or soft words that drew her to comply, but she lifted her skirts a little and extended her legs to show her feet. He ripped what remained of her stockings and pulled the material aside. She gasped at the sudden movement and loud tearing sound. With a gentle touch, he raked his thumb around the inflamed areas, jolting her upright.

"This could get infected. I'll get bandages and clean the wounds. You need to rest tonight. Tomorrow, I'll take you to Prairie City and you'll be on your way."

This man could say whatever he wanted, but Abigail wasn't going anywhere. She'd fight to make this land work, to get her sisters out of their desperate situation back in Georgia. Despite his assurances that this was no land for women, she and her sisters could do this. They could do anything, so long as they were together.

She yawned. Her head felt like a cannon ball about to tumble from her neck. The warm air in the small one-room structure made her eyes grow heavy, and she rested her head on her arm for a moment before it slipped and smacked the tabletop.

He chuckled. "I'll fix you some food. Then you should get some rest before you fall down." Examining her feet again, he asked, "Whatever made you walk from Gardner in these shoes?"

"The coach ride took a day longer than I had expected, and when my cousin didn't meet me at the station, I thought he had given up hope that I'd arrive. There was no way to contact him either, and no coach would come to this area." She shrugged. "So I walked. Nothing will stop me from making this work. Not my feet, not some squatter, and not the harshness of this land."

Owen shook his head then held a finger in front of her face. "One day. One day out here and you'll be begging to return to Georgia. Trust me."

Too tired to argue the point, she said nothing. While she still didn't like the idea of relying on a man, she realized he'd be useful to have around until she got the hang of things here. In the morning, she'd convince him to help her build up her new land so she could bring her sisters over as soon as possible. Once the seven of them were back together, she'd get him to leave. Relying on a man anymore than absolutely necessary wasn't going to happen again. Ever.

Chapter Three

Owen struggled to fall asleep. The pile of straw he'd been using for a bed never had been comfortable, but after moving it outside under the bright moon, with the wild dogs howling in the distance, he was having even more trouble relaxing. He could move to the barn and put the ox outside, but he preferred the open air to the smell of animals. Not to mention the flies. Who was he kidding? The beautiful woman sleeping inside churned up all sorts of emotions. He knew homesteading would be lonely, but with Willy gone, he'd be facing complete solitude. If he was honest with himself, the first glance at the red-haired woman stumbling over the hill made his heart lurch for something he once had, or thought he would have.

His courtship with Emma was quick, their marriage even quicker. Within less than a week he'd gone from bachelor to husband to widower. He'd only married the girl and taken on her son as his own to save her from the scorn of her ken folk. But never again. He was done taking on charity cases. He wasn't going to try to save some woman from her circumstances only to put her in an even worse situation.

For hours, he tossed and turned, thinking about his options until the sun rose and shot sparks of orange and yellow across the pale sky. The crisp, clean morning air entered his lungs like a creek bath, invigorating him. Life here was hard and lonely, but it didn't matter. It took him far away from the noises of the city.

He rose, brushed the straw from his pants and then checked on Ms. McKinnie. Drawing back the sheet Willy had strung across the doorway more to block the heat of the day than for privacy, he stepped softly over to the bed. The wounds on her feet had oozed through the bandages during the night. He'd have to re-bandage them once she woke up. Her reddish hair fell in waves around her face, her pale skin now red with sunburn. Even in rags and with her disheveled appearance and bloodied feet, she was the most entrancing woman he'd ever seen. He could stand there for hours and just watch her soft breaths, the slight rise and fall of her chest, her parted lips.

He shook his head. *Fool.* He always did have a soft spot for a woman in need. He had to get Ms. McKinnie out of here and quick, before he subjected another innocent to the harshness of this land.

With bucket in hand, he filled it at the well and carried it to the barn to check on the only occupant, Willy's plow ox. The barn was so small it only fit one animal at a time. By winter, he'd have to expand it to get his horse out of the pasture. After filling the feed and water bins, he headed over to work on the windmill he and Willy had been building when Willy fell. It hadn't been the fall that killed the poor man, but a fever he'd caught from his injuries. The doc said there was nothin' that could've been done. He hated that helpless feeling.

He worked for hours, checking on Ms. McKinnie several times, hoping to drive her into town before it got too late, but the woman continued to sleep. He even made some noise at one point, in hopes of startling her awake, but nothing would stir her. She was either more exhausted than she'd let on or she was darn good at faking.

He spent the entire day working on the windmill, adjusting the blades, connecting the shafts and gears to the pump mechanism. Having the windmill up and running would save him from carrying water out to the barn for the ox and horse daily. Not to mention it would be essential once he got the fields plowed and planted. As the sun fell in the sky his stomach rumbled with hunger and he decided to head to the house.

Wind swept through the prairie, stirring up dust. He wiped his face free of dirt and sweat before he realized he smelled something. Something good. He quickened his pace and found Ms. McKinnie stoking the fire in the wood stove. The small dugout sweltered with the heat of the stove, but the hearty smell of meat welcomed him into his home. “What you doing?”

She blew her hair out of her face and straightened, wiping her hands down the front of her dress and giving him an are-you-stupid look. “I’m plowing a field.”

Dang, she was sassy, not the sweet-talking, sensitive type he’d expected. “Yeah, I can see that.” He ran his rag over the back of his neck and scooted closer to her, spotting salted meat in the cast iron pan along with some eggs.

"You get them eggs from my chickens?" He quirked a brow at her. Emma had refused to even touch a chicken. Not that she had much time to acclimate to country life before she fell ill.

"My property, my chickens." She flipped the eggs, waited a minute, then slid chunks of meat and two eggs onto a tin plate and then the remaining portion onto the other plate.

"About that... I'll give you the amount Mr. O'Brien bought the place for when I take you into town. I'm not gonna be able to pay what the land's worth right now, but I can pay you some to help you get home."

"Nonsense. Don't be daft. If anyone's leaving it's going to be you." She handed him a plate then grabbed her own, tucked the curtain out of the way on the hook, and settled on a stump outside the doorway.

Sighing, he turned to follow her. "Listen, I don't have time to care for you, or worry about you getting injured. I've wasted too much time already. I need to get this field turned so I can plant next season. And I haven't even started preparing for winter. I need to gather wood or I'm gonna freeze." He knocked a knuckle against the doorframe. "Not to mention building a door for the front of my house."

"My house," she said without looking up.

He placed his hat on the hook and analyzed the food on his plate. It would be great to have someone cook for him. Always spending long days working around the homestead, he was often too exhausted to bother cooking anything. And going into Prairie City for a good meal took too much time. "You won't survive out here by yourself. I'll have to take care of you."

"As far as I can tell, I'm taking care of you." She took a few dainty bites, like a Southern belle at a tea party, before she pointed a finger at his food.

"I could've…you didn't need to…" Sighing, he said, "Fine. So, you can cook, but I don't need a wife to take care of me."

"Wife? You presume too much, sir." She rose on her bandaged feet and lifted her chin proudly. "I do not need, nor do I wish for a husband, so you need not concern yourself. If marriage is what's concerning you, let me relieve it for you now. I am not your responsibility. I only wish to use what my cousin owned and build a life for myself here. I will do my work. From now on, you may cook for yourself if that is what you wish."

How'd this woman turn his words around so completely? He quirked a brow at her. "You're telling me you don't want a husband? You came all the way out here, even walked twenty miles, just to marry Willy. Now you're saying you don't want a husband? You running away from something?" He stared at her for a moment. "You know what? I don't want to know. I'm no savior, lady."

"And I never asked you to be. I can save myself, thank you. All you men do is fight. I prefer to do things for myself." She set her plate down on the table then propped her hands on her hips. "Let's settle this now. Are the chickens yours or mine?"

"We purchased them together. We were going to split them up once we grew our first crops so we'd have money to buy our own."

"Fine, we share, but you cook your own eggs. The ox and plow?"

"Shared."

She blew out an exasperated breath. "Is there anything that belonged solely to Mr. O'Brien on this land?"

He shook his head. "That's what I've been trying to tell you. No one can take on this prairie land alone. No one. Willy purchased the land but was about to abandon it and move back to town when I came through. I purchased the adjacent homestead so we could work together." He gestured toward the barn, well, and shed. "We only made it this far by working together. Even with all this already established, a woman won't last a week trying to plow, fetch water, build fires, and find food by herself. Don't forget your feet are blistered, you're sunburned, and weak from your travels. You think the animals can just wait until you're well-rested and healed? And what about coyotes and wolves? You think you can fend off a pack of wolves by yourself, too?"

He was positive the fear of a wolf attack would wise her up and she'd be begging him to take her back to town. Yet, she only stared at him for a moment. Then she bent down, retrieved his food, shoved her skirts to the side and paraded to the wash bucket. "You already admitted the house is mine. You step foot inside and I'll consider that trespassing. You can sleep outside or in the barn from now on. Let's see if you can last a week."

His temper reared faster than a spooked horse. "I was born to work this land. I admit it'll be hard, but I don't need any help from some Southern woman with a high and mighty attitude. No wonder your kind lost the war."

She swung around on him, getting right in his face, and he stumbled back a few steps. The fierceness in her eyes, the trembling of her lip, the hatred in her stance all made him wish he'd kept his temper under control. "You know nothing of war. You probably fled west so you didn't have to serve. Well, I stayed. I endured the bombardment of cannons. I survived the fires. My sisters and I paid for that war in blood and tears and lives. You have no idea what I've been through. Don't ever think you're tougher than me, just because you're a man." Her eyes narrowed with the threat of a wild animal about to attack. "By the end of this week, I'll drive you from *my* land."

For the next week, Mr. Baker would go out to work on the windmill while she churned butter, gathered eggs, and cooked. There was little to no conversation between them. What was left to say? He didn't want her there, and she wasn't leaving. By the seventh day, she had enough of him insisting her feet needed to heal before she did anything more strenuous, so she dressed in the clothes she'd brought with her and got to work. Just seeing the clothes stirred fresh grief at her brother's death. He would never wear them again, never nag her for being unladylike again.

Even though her brother was skinny, she still had to synch the waist tight with a belt and stuff material into the toes of his work boots so they wouldn't flop off when she walked. At least it was putting her destroyed dress to good use. She was never going to wear it again anyway.

She stepped out into the open air and scanned the landscape for any signs of Mr. Baker lurking nearby. With no sign of his large frame, she made her way to the shed. Having learned her lesson after that twenty-mile trek in the sun, this time, she tugged her bonnet over her head to shield her face from the sun's burning rays.

If only she could make Mr. Baker listen. She would've been willing to keep him on as hired help, but not after his repeated attempts to convince her she was nothing more than a weak, helpless female. They could've already sent for her sisters, but at this rate there wouldn't be any more food or resources than what they had in Georgia. Her heart ached at the thought that it had been a week since she'd even been able to send a letter to them. She'd written ten or so already, but with no way to mail them, they sat on the table inside the small house.

The plow was kept inside the shed, along with most of the planting supplies. Abigail managed to wrench it free of its dirt resting place in the corner where it seemed to have been for some time. Once outside, she checked again that the coast was clear.

The man would no doubt try to stop her if he found out what she was doing. But thankfully, there was no sign of him. Like every day for the last week, he'd probably reappear sometime around evening when hunger called.

After hitching the ox to the plow, she flung the leather strap behind her and began to clear the spread of land near the animal pen figuring if the dugout was on her property this field had to be, too. She'd have to ask him later to show her the property lines. Hidden rocks and the dense root system of the prairie grass proved more arduous than the soil back home. This land was alive, but challenged her to give up and return home with its constant obstacles.

Several hours into the sweaty, dirty, exhausting task, she wanted to release the handles of the plow and crawl back to the dugout where she'd beg Mr. Baker to take her to the train station, but that wasn't an option. Other than her sisters, there was nothing left for her in Georgia. Their plantation was destroyed, their land now useless. Her parents and brothers were gone. No, she had to do everything she could to build a new life for her sisters here.

She stopped long enough to eat a little bread and drink some water in the shade of the barn when the sun sat hottest overhead. Perhaps she could cool off in the creak and allow the muscles in her back that screamed in discomfort a break. Not to mention her hands. Aching and blistered, they now matched how her feet looked that first day. Yet, she knew there wasn't time. She needed to get the land cleared and set for planting before winter hit. With each day that passed, the temperature dropped in warning.

In the days that followed, she awoke after Mr. Baker had already left to the upper fields. She'd rise, dress, hitch the ox up and plow her field. On the fourth day, her blisters bled, the stinging pain hitting with a severity she hadn't expected, and she decided to quit early for the day. On the way back to the house after putting the plow away, she checked one of the traps she had set, the way her eldest brother had taught her. To her surprise, it had caught a jack rabbit. It wasn't much, but she could make stew for lunch. To think that at one time she thought she could never do such a thing, that the task of skinning and cooking something she'd caught herself was too barbaric and gruesome. But that was before the war, before she had to watch her dear sisters starve. So she ignored her nature and became another person. A person willing to do anything to save her family.

Just as the stew was ready, she heard the sound of wood being chopped, Mr. Baker's late afternoon activity. Tired of the silence between them, she poured stew into two bowls, deciding she'd offer some to Mr. Baker as a peace offering. Perhaps he'd be more amenable once he had a real meal in his belly.

She rounded the dugout and spotted Mr. Baker by the wood pile, his shirt draped over a log. His tan muscles exposed, they tightened and released along his back and shoulders with each swing of the axe. She'd never seen a man working with his shirt off before. Not a man that would draw her attention anyway. But *he* drew her attention. There was no doubt about that. She had to force her gaping mouth closed, yet she refused to drop her gaze. She wouldn't give him the chance to think her some simpering female. She cleared her throat. "I have lunch. Rabbit stew. Not much, but you're welcome to it."

Mr. Baker lodged his axe into the log and adjusted his hat. "One of your traps worked?"

She didn't know that he was aware of her traps. What else was he aware of? "Of course it worked."

He looked over his shoulder with a mischievous grin, but then turned and fixed his gaze on her as though analyzing something. "What are you wearing?" he asked.

"You're aware of the traps but just noticing that?" She laughed, a delicate, happy sound she hadn't let escape in years. "Not perceptive, are you? I've been in these same clothes all week. I only had the one dress, and I can't work in that. Not to mention it's only worthy of rags at this point." She spun on her heels and headed back inside the dugout. After placing the bowls on the table, she grabbed the bucket and walked to the well to fetch more water, but the rope fibers cut into her raw skin and she dropped it with a thud on the ground.

Mr. Baker was at her side an instant later. Before she could hide her blistered hands, he grabbed her by the wrists and yanked them from her sides. "Jesus, Mary, and Joseph! What have you done to yourself?"

She snatched her arms back and squared her shoulders. "Just a few blisters. I'm fine. Nothing I didn't expect to get while working my land."

He removed his hat and smacked it against his leg. "Woman, what are you doing to yourself? Why?" He shook his head and ran a hand through his thick, dark hair. His blue eyes darted left and right as if he was searching for something. He paced back and forth, mumbling inaudibly until he turned to her. “It’s time you listened to me.”

Before she managed to say a word, he swept her up and carried her inside the dugout, placing her gently on the bed. “Don’t move, or I swear I’ll tie you to that chair over there.” She gasped at his forcefulness, but quickly recovered. She eyed him but didn’t argue. Something told her he’d do whatever it took to keep her still, and any arguing would only make him haul her back to town tied to a chair. So, she decided to play this out until he went back to the upper field. She’d learned things were always easier if she avoided arguing with Mr. Baker and just did what she wanted when he wasn’t around.

After several minutes, he returned with cold, damp rags and gingerly pressed them to her blistered palms. The sting took her breath away, but she gritted her teeth and tried to keep her screams of discomfort from escaping.

“Why do you do these things to yourself, woman?”

“I’m not *woman*. My name is Abigail. And *I’m* doing this because it’s my land. Who else is going to do the work if I just sit sewing?”

He chuckled, his gaze dipping over her from neck to knees. “Oh, you’re a woman all right. The most stubborn one to ever walk this prairie.” She huffed and pulled at her arm, but he wouldn’t let her go. “Stay still.” He dabbed at the oozing blisters then his shoulders lowered into a more relaxed posture. “You’re crazy. I don’t know many men who could plow as much land as you have these last few days, but you need to know your limits. Or you’ll end up putting yourself into that ground instead of seeds.”

His hands were gentle despite the roughness of his skin. Releasing his determined grip, he retrieved the jar of ointment he’d used on her feet and applied it with light touches of the rag. How could a man be so compassionate one minute and such an overbearing jerk the next? As much as he refused to leave, he had still cared for her injuries. He also slept outside, leaving her with the dugout.

She dared to run her fingers over his hand to still his movements. “Why won’t you relent and understand I’m not leaving?”

He paused, his mouth open for a moment before words finally came out. “You don’t belong here.” He finished bandaging her hands and then stood. “Stay put.”

She didn't listen and stood to finish her evening chores, but he invaded her space, causing her to stumble back from his massive frame and narrowed gaze.

"I swear, woman, I will tie you up, put you over my horse and take you to town this minute, kicking and screaming if I have to, if you don't stay in bed the rest of the day."

Abigail didn't know if it was his determined stare, or his twitching jaw, but she knew he meant it. "Fine, but in the morning, I'm back to plowing."

He shook his head and dropped the rags onto the floor. "You're done plowing."

Before she could reply, he disappeared out the doorway, letting the curtain swing back into place, and she was alone again. The remaining daylight hours proved more strenuous than plowing fields as loneliness plagued her. She missed the sounds of bickering from her little sisters, conversations with Cora, managing the plantation and dealing with neighbors. Here, there was no one to talk to except for a man who only said three or four words at a time, usually to bark orders or dismiss her.

She attempted to write a letter, but her hands couldn't hold her pen long enough to scribble a legible word. For hours, she sat on the stump outside, watching the prairie grass blow in the wind, listening to the horse neigh, the chickens cluck, and the wind whistle. Clouds rolled in during the late afternoon with the dark promise of rain. Perhaps it would moisten the soil, making it easier to plow.

Night drew near and Mr. Baker returned. He made dinner in silence while she sat on the bed and watched. He set a plate on the table and directed her to sit. Wind blew through the curtain, and she couldn't help but think about how exposed they were to the harsh world outside. "Perhaps we can make a door for the dugout soon."

He didn't answer. He only scooped runny eggs onto a fork and held them up for her to take a bite. At the gross, uncooked consistency, she wondered how he'd survived his own cooking before she arrived. "Sorry, I'm good with land, not with cookin'."

She smiled. "Well, that's one thing we can agree on." For the first time in days, he snickered. It was the first sign of happiness she'd seen in him since arriving here. "That's nice."

"What?" He scooped another forkful and she took it without complaint.

"You smiled, and almost laughed. It's okay to enjoy life once in a while, you know." She nudged her knee into his.

He shoveled the last of the eggs into her mouth with less care then took the plate. "This doesn't change anything. I hope you see now that you don't belong here."

She shoved her chair back, tipping it to the ground. "I'm not leaving."

He only shook his head and left the dugout. For hours, she sat in silence once more, except for the thunder rolling in like cannon fire. She hated the sound, one she wished never to hear again. She paced the small room until she couldn't take the sound any longer, or the thought of Mr. Baker sleeping outside in that kind of weather, even though he deserved it.

As she rushed to the doorway, the curtain blew open and she caught a glimpse of the man huddled close to the dugout, trying to stay dry. Inviting him in would be a good gesture, especially after he had tended to her wounds. Perhaps it would give her another opportunity to convince him she wasn't leaving and get his help to deliver her letters to Prairie City. If she didn't get word to them soon,

Chapter Five

Owen changed out of his wet clothes while Abigail faced the back dirt wall of the dugout. Thunder rolled, warning of an even bigger storm to come. He only hoped the twisters wouldn't hit. One of those monsters could destroy everything he and Willy had worked so hard to build in a matter of seconds. At least they were as safe as they could be in the dugout.

"You can turn around now." He buttoned his shirt and sat at the table. "Have any stew left?"

She shook her head and sat across from him. "No, we ate it all. I'm sure I'll have more fresh meat within a few days though. I also hope to start a garden for some vegetables come spring. Probably be a good idea to build a root cellar, too."

Owen leaned back in the chair, stretching his aching muscles. How could Abigail still move after all the labor she'd been putting in these last days? "How you feeling?"

She lifted her chin and sat straight as a pine tree. "Fine."

He didn't want it to be this way between them, but he needed her to see she couldn't stay. "If you keep working like this, you're going to end up ill. If I promise not to put you on my horse tomorrow, will you promise to take another day to rest? Even God rested after his work was done."

Her shoulders relaxed and she smiled, a sweet smile that melted his heart. He wanted to see that more often. They remained silent for a few minutes listening to the rain before he managed to think of something else to say. "Speaking of God, you want to go into town for church on Sunday?"

She thought for a moment, but then shook her head. "I don't think it would be proper for me to attend church with a man who isn't my husband. Besides, I don't have any material to make a dress."

"I'm surprised you didn't bring more. Don't women usually travel with trunks?"

She sighed. "I used to travel north quite often with two trunks full of dresses and thought I didn't have enough. But then the war broke out." She squirmed and her shoulders sunk. "Most of our house was burned to the ground. Our kitchen and parlor were the only parts of the house left standing. Luckily, when they set fire to a wagon of cotton, it tipped over and burned out. We were able to salvage most of that load and spin it into linen. We used some and sold the rest to buy food."

He scooted closer. "I'm sorry you lost so much in the war." He dug his nail into a crack in the wood tabletop and traced the line. "I left before the war had broken out. I couldn't serve on the North or South side. Not when my two brothers were split. I knew I couldn't face either on the field and kill them."

Abigail's pink lips dropped open with a small sigh. "I don't understand. Certainly both brothers served the same purpose."

He shrugged. "I left home at the age of twelve, lived in the Missouri territory for a while working odd jobs. I didn't have a mind for schooling, and I didn't want to take over my father's business. One of my brothers went north to study and the other married and started his own farm near where my parents once lived in Virginia." Owen fought the lump rising in his throat, wanting to avoid his memories of his brothers. "When war broke out, my parents wanted to take my sister away from the turmoil back home, so my father moved the family business to St. Joseph near me."

Her fingers brushed over his knuckles, stopping nail digging into the table. "What happened to your brothers?"

He swallowed the pain of loss and forced the words out. "Died on the frontline. I only hope they never faced each other in battle." He didn't like talking about his brothers, but he didn't want to pull his hand away and close up again either. The softness of her fingers reached beyond his skin into a spot inside him he'd forgotten about. The way a woman's touch could raise a man up and make him feel like he could do anything.

Moments passed without a word then she settled back in her chair, taking her connection with her. He wanted more from her, but hated himself for it. As much as instinct and need drove him to care for another woman, he knew he couldn't handle the consequences of that selfish decision. Not again.

Pushing away from the table, he snagged the dishes and went to clean them in the large bucket beside the wood stove. He knew if he left them for too long, she would only try to clean them herself and she shouldn't get her wounds wet. He needed to get away from her. Storm or no storm, it was safer for him outside than in that small space with a woman as beautiful as Abigail McKinnie. With her long red hair tussled around her face, her green eyes that mesmerized him with their brilliant shine, and her lips, she was more dangerous than a pack of wolves. Were her lips as soft as they looked? He rinsed the plates and headed for the doorway.

Two rolls of thunder sounded.

"Do you go to church on Sundays?"

Her words stopped him from the insanity of sleeping outside on a night like this. "I did when Willy was alive. Well, most Sundays," he pointed toward the curtain, "when there was good weather."

She edged back in her seat and placed her hands on the table instead of hidden in her lap. "You should go. I'll be fine here."

A clap of thunder sounded again and she jolted.

He eyed her tense posture. "Storms get pretty fierce out here sometimes."

The wind whipped the curtain, threatening to shred it to pieces, so he tacked it down before turning to face her again. Seeing her trembling at the table, he asked, "You cold?"

"No. I'm fine." She stood and turned down the kerosene lamp. "We should get some sleep." Before he could respond, she crawled into bed, but even under the weight of the blanket he could see her shaking.

He retrieved his blanket from his trunk and draped it over her despite the warm night. *Dear God, please don't let her be sick.* He pressed a hand to her forehead and she jolted. "I'm just checking your temperature." Her skin felt cold and clammy.

She brushed his hand away. "I'm fine."

Thunder echoed across the prairie, pounding the ground beneath his feet. She yelped and squished herself against the wall. He dropped to his knees by the bed and stroked her hair away from her delicate, perfect face. "What is it?"

"I told you I'm fine," her voice cracked with fear.

"Talk to me. How can I help? It's the thunder, right?"

She didn't respond. No surprise there. He'd created this tension between them. He'd done everything but what he'd threatened to do—tie her up and throw her over his horse to take her back to town. He'd been barbaric and rude. Even if he knew she had to leave, he couldn't bear to see her like this. "Have you always been scared of storms?"

"I'm not scared of storms." Another clap and she covered her ears. "Make it stop. Make them stop."

"Them?"

She rocked and hummed in a manic way.

Pulling her toward him, he cradled her in his arms. She resisted at first but froze with the next thunder clap. Her heart raced as if it would jump from her chest. "Shh. It's all right. Everything is gonna be all right." The thunder rattled the dishes and shook the earth around them. He pressed his lips to the top of her head to sooth her. Even after all the work she'd put in, and only being able to bathe a few times, her hair still smelled like fresh wild flowers. The fragrance suited her wild temperament.

She continued to whimper, curling into him, clinging to him, clawing at him to hold her tighter, and he obliged. *Lord above, help me*, he thought. He liked the feel of this woman against his chest, and even more he wanted to protect her, to care for her. The one thing he didn't want in his life again. He couldn't bear to watch another woman die.

The storm died down and she finally relaxed against him, falling to sleep in his arms. He angled himself so he could cradle her while he slept, too.

But when the storm revved back to life a few hours later, she screamed, “Hide! They’re coming!”

He steadied her in his arms and stroked her hair. Her eyes were half-glazed with sleep, but the dark pupils had nearly conquered the green of her eyes. “I’m here. No one’s coming.”

“They are! They’re coming! They already hurt my baby sister. They killed my little brother. They burned our fields and home, and now they’re coming to take more from us.” She pushed from his arms and tried to scramble away, but he grabbed hold and wrapped his arms around her to keep her at his side.

“You’re safe.”

“I’m supposed to protect them. That’s my job as the eldest, and I’m going to fail them,” she sobbed. A whispered name broke from her lips before Abigail bolted from the bed and ran out into the rain.

Josephine?

He chased after her into the heart of the storm. Lightning chinked across the sky, hitting the ground in the distance. Sparks erupted but quickly died under the fierce rain. “Abigail, stop!”

The wind whirled her hair in a fiery inferno of gold and red shining in the lightening flash. He caught hold of her and spun her in his arms. With a tighter grip than he liked to use on a woman, he held her against him, fearful she'd stumble into the darkness beyond his reach. Another flash of lightning streaked the night sky, illuminating her face, and he saw it. The expression he'd seen on many men over the years. The same fear-filled gaze that screamed she'd seen the horrors of war.

Abigail awoke the next morning to a pounding in her head, the previous night only a foggy memory. The dugout's silence told her she was alone. She sat up and realized she was dressed in a long shirt. *His* long shirt. Frantically searching her memory for details, she grasped the full extent of what happened last night. Her screams and ranting, the rain, her only set of clothes soaked through. It had been months since she had an episode, but nonetheless, it happened.

Once he'd calmed her, he gave her clothes and ordered her to change and rest. With heat rising to her cheeks, she snagged her brother's pants and shirt from the table where they lay drying and dressed. A note on the table caught her attention.

I rode into town for supplies. I'll be back by evening. Please rest.

Owen

P.S. If I catch you attempting to plow, or do any other manual labor, you'll be on the next train home.

Well, gardening or trapping couldn't really be considered manual labor, so Abigail headed out to check her traps and then began tending to the small garden she'd planted with the seedlings Mr. O'Brien had started several months before he died. If she couldn't plow the fields on her own before the harsh winter made the ground too hard to work, she needed to prove she could trade for Owen's help.

The sound of horse hooves told her Owen was back, so she raced around the side of the barn to find a woman, clothed in a simple dress and bonnet, atop a horse. "Good morning," the woman said, pulling the horse to a stop. Dismounting by sliding off the side, she straightened her skirt then held out a hand. "I'm Susan Dunst." She had a strange smile, one of curiosity and happiness, and an even stranger accent. One of half a life spent in a far off place, and half a life in the country. "Where's Mr. Baker?"

Abigail glanced down at her own clothing and worried the woman might faint at her attire. "He went to town. Sorry about this, but I wasn't expecting anyone and the dress I have isn't practical for working in."

"I see." Susan wrapped the horse's bridle around a post. "No judgment from me. I wished I would've thought of it. Dresses aren't conducive to hard labor or riding horseback. And prairie life is full of hard labor. I can see you've already discovered that part though." She pointed to the dry blood and blisters on Abigail's hands.

Instinctively, Abigail shoved them into her pockets.

The woman's skin was tan and lined, no doubt from years of work in the sun. She had a stronger frame than most women Abigail knew, yet she still held herself like a lady. "You here with Mr. Baker? He send for you like my husband suggested?"

"Sent for me?" Abigail lifted an eyebrow at her.

Susan half-laughed, half-sputtered. "No, he wouldn't do that."

Abigail sighed. "I came here for my cousin, Willy O'Brien. Unfortunately, he passed away before I arrived. Now, I own his land." She jutted out her chin and pushed her shoulders back, ready for an argument. That was all she got from Owen whenever she said this was her land.

Susan clapped her hand against her hip. "Good for you."

Clouds rolled over the sun, shading them so Abigail didn't have to squint any longer. She smiled. "Glad you think so. Mr. Baker's not so keen on me staying. Says I don't belong here. After last night, I wouldn't be surprised if he showed up with a deed to this property and a train ticket for me to return to Georgia."

"Last night?" Susan's voice dipped with concern.

Abigail looked around and realized the misunderstanding. From Susan's perspective, she was an unmarried woman sharing a one room dugout with a man. "Oh, nothing like that. I mean, he sleeps outside. I sleep inside. Nothing improper here, I assure you. Well, except last night." Her thoughts the conundrum that was Owen Baker, a man who ordered her away one minute, scolded her the next, and then held her in his arms afterward. "What I mean is—"

"Not to worry, my dear. I didn't think anything improper was going on with Mr. Baker. He's a fine man. I'm more concerned about the storm. Was there a fire?"

"Oh, no. I, um, I'm not good with storms. I'll get better, though." Abigail felt heat surge into her cheeks again. "Must sound childish to you. The thunder just reminds me of the war."

Susan tucked strands of loose hair into her bonnet. "I see. And you think he wants you gone because he wants the property for himself?"

Abigail shrugged. "That, and he believes I'm too weak to handle prairie life." She'd been so starved for female interaction the words rolled from her mouth faster than a jackrabbit ran from a wolf.

Susan held up a finger by her ear. "Ah, I see. Have you been out past the south pasture yet?"

"No. I've been busy plowing the field over by the barn. Mr. Baker's been working on windmills up there though."

The clouds parted and sun beat down on them once again. "If you have some time, I'd love to walk with you," Susan offered. "You'll find life out here can get a little lonely, especially for a woman. And I have something to show you that'll help you understand Mr. Baker a little better. I wouldn't mind getting to know you better, too. You're the closest female neighbor I have."

Already Abigail liked Susan. She had a strength about her Abigail had never seen before.

Perhaps she could learn some things from Susan that would help with her life on the prairie. “That would be wonderful. Mr. Baker made me promise not to plow, threatening to tie me to a horse and drive me back to the closest train station. And I am not going back. It took me too long to get here.”

Susan laughed then guided her out toward the south pasture. “Ah, rough trip? Did you travel by coach or train?

They waded through the tall prairie grass and up the hill. “I thought traveling by train would be the better option, but after General Sherman burned lands, bent tracks, and blew up bridges, you can only travel so far by rail right now.” She fought the rise of hate filling her. “I had to change trains several times, and travel part of the way by ferry and coach. I ended up walking the last stretch.”

Susan shook her head. “I heard of much destruction with his march to the sea. I’m glad you escaped the worst of it and you’re here with us now. It might be a tough life, but it’s full of promise.” She winked. “I like to say that there is hope in the prairie dust.” Susan’s smile and words buffed the edges of Abigail’s mood down to her normal softness.

They broke free of the tall, brown grass and crested the small hill. A large tree with several branches provided welcomed shade. Three crosses pierced the ground beneath the tree where grass no longer grew. She walked over and eyed the names scratched into the wood. *Willy O'Brien. Emma Sue Baker. Thomas Baker.* "Who were they?"

Susan touched her fingers to her lips then pressed them to the top of the cross marking Thomas Baker's final resting place. "Willy O'Brien you know. The others were friends. A wife and child."

Abigail gasped. "Owen—I mean, Mr. Baker was married and had a child?"

Susan bit her bottom lip as if to contemplate how to share the story of Owen Baker. "He was married, briefly, to Emma Sue. Poor girl had a tough run of luck, what with an abusive father and brother. From what my husband, Martin, tells me, Owen married Emma Sue to save her from that life. Not that he didn't care for her. I'm sure he did, but their courtship was brief, and their marriage even shorter."

Abigail sucked in a long breath of fresh air, as if breathing in reality for the first time since arriving at the homestead. "And the child?"

"The child was Emma Sue's from a previous marriage. Owen left the wagon train he was part of when his wife and child became too sick to travel. He was taking them to Prairie City for medical care, but both she and the boy died on the way. That's when Owen met Willy. Giving up his dream of heading out to California, Owen bought the adjacent property and he and Willy agreed to work together to make their homesteads thrive."

Abigail nodded. "Mr. Baker had mentioned something about that." Her heart twitched with regret for the way she'd lashed out at Owen, but what choice did she have? She needed the land more than he did. She still had a family to take care of, a family that needed her help desperately.

Susan eyed the horizon and then the dugout in the distance. "I know I shouldn't meddle, but I thought you should know about his past before you gave up on him. Try to give him a chance to come around."

"Give him a chance?" she asked. Then it hit her. "Oh, no. I'm not trying to woo Mr. Baker. I'm not interested in finding a husband at all. I just want to work my land and build a life here so I can bring my sisters out. Once I can build a home large enough for all of us to live in, I will send for them."

Susan slid her arm into the crook of Abigail's and they headed back down the hill. "I'm afraid wood is scarce in these parts, especially after the Indians burned most of the forests. Lumber can be purchased in town, but it's expensive and you need a wagon to transport it. Owen's property is on the other side of the creek, and there's still plenty of trees there, but you'll need to be cautious. It's close to Indian territory, and they aren't the friendly kind of Indians either."

They reached Susan's horse and to Abigail's surprise she was sad for Susan to be leaving. It had been so long since she had another person to talk to, the way she had with her sisters back home. "I hope you'll come visit again soon."

Susan untethered her horse and pulled the reins over its head. Tightening her bonnet, she said, "I would like that. Here. I brought some bread for Mr. Baker, along with some apples and flour." She untied a bag from the saddle horn and handed it to Abigail. "Don't be too mad at Owen. I think he just doesn't want to face the possibility of losing someone else. Since Willy passed, we hadn't heard from him. Of course, we didn't know he had any company. We used to meet up to trade supplies at least once every few days. But at the burial, he told my husband he wouldn't bother us in the future, which meant he was planning to live out here with no one to look in on him. I think he tried to distance himself so he wouldn't have to watch another person die."

Abigail's pulse quickened. "Are you?"

"No, I'm fine. That's just prairie life. It's rough out here, but I think you can handle it. Don't let him run you off now." She steered the horse toward the trail Owen had said led to the city. "Mr. Baker's a good man," Susan called over her shoulder. "He'd make a fine husband."

Prairie City boomed with more activity than he'd remembered, as if the population had tripled since the last time he'd come into town. Wagons barreled through the streets full of goods from one of the two general stores. After finishing up his order at the saw mill, he found the claim's office closed, so he headed to Mr. Graham's General Store for supplies.

Scantily-clad women stood in the doorway of a saloon at the end of the street next to the store. Owen hopped down off the buck board, tethered his horse, and tipped his hat to two women waving him over, but he ignored their summons and continued into the store. Saloons were his older brothers' thing, not his.

He entered the store, eager to finish his business in town and return with the wood he'd purchased to start building a better home on his property. He was fine in the dugout, but he wouldn't mooch off anyone. Perhaps he'd keep the dugout and give the new house to Abigail, if he couldn't get her to leave. He'd build on the edge of his property near the dugout.

Mr. Graham finished with a client then dusted off the remnants of sugar on the counter before greeting Owen. "Hi, Mr. Baker. How's the homestead coming along? I was so sorry to hear about Mr. O'Brien. God rest his soul."

Owen eyed the dresses on display in the window of the store he'd remembered seeing the last time he rode into town to get supplies. "Yes, he was a good man."

Mr. Graham nodded and hurried over to the farming equipment. "We received the newest plows in last week."

The door opened with a jingle and several giggling women entered. Owen eyed the dress of the first girl, her hair tucked into a matching pink bonnet, before he realized he was staring. "Sorry, ma'am."

She fanned her face as if embarrassed but then edged closer. "That's all right, sir. I know prairie life can be lonely without a wife. My poor Jake took to the fever two months ago, so I know what you've been through."

The promising tone in her voice told Owen he better scoot before he found himself getting hitched again. "I'm sorry for your loss, ma'am," he said before turning back to Mr. Graham. "The claims office was closed. Do you know when Johnson will be back? I have some questions."

"He had to go to Kansas City for a family issue. He should be returning in a few days." Mr. Graham pointed to a jar on a nearby shelf. "Got some great tobacco."

The group of women crowded around a shelf of hats, whispering to one another. The girl with the pink bonnet smiled, her gaze following him as he moved about the store. Owen didn't understand the woman's attention. It wasn't like she didn't have her pick of the men in town. Heck, there were probably ten men to every woman in these parts.

Owen moved closer to Mr. Graham and tilted his head toward the dress hanging next to the bolts of fabric in the front of the store. "Is that what women folk wear for farming?"

Mr. Graham's eyes lit up at the potential sale. He was a nice man, unlike his judgmental wife loitering nearby to hear all the latest gossip, but he was a salesman to the bone. "Did you get married?"

That certainly perked the ears of the pink bonnet woman and her two friends, Mrs. Graham, and anyone else within earshot. Owen focused on a knot in the floorboard beneath his feet. "No. It's for O'Brien's bride."

"I didn't know he got married." Mrs. Graham abandoned her task and nudged in between Mr. Graham and the counter to get a front row seat to Owen's discomfort. "Poor thing. Where's she living now that O'Brien's gone?"

"She's at the homestead, but she needs some clothes."

"She's naked?" The woman with the pink bonnet now looked shocked and horrified. Her dark-haired friend clung to her side with her mouth hung open and eyes wide.

"No, ma'am, but her dress was ruined by her travels." Owen had to think quick about how to handle this without creating anymore gossip. "I'm working on sending her back to Georgia where she came from."

"But she's living out in that one room dugout...alone with you?" Mrs. Graham's fingers fiddled with the lace around her neck, her pudgy face turning red.

The woman with the pink bonnet swooned. "Dear Lord, how scandalous."

"Well, I never." The dark-haired woman took her by the arm and all three of them retreated outside as if his words were too inappropriate for their ears.

How'd this get so out of control? "It's not like I want her there. And I'm not living in the dugout. It's all perfectly proper, ma'am. I assure you. Abigail McKinnie is a lady of fine breeding, and possesses the most upright character."

Mr. Graham shooed his wife away. "Do you want to ruin our business? Go away, woman." He retrieved the printed dresses with lots of little flowers and a bonnet. "This would be perfect for around the homestead and riding into town. This is a sample of an everyday dress one of the widows made, but I can sell it to you. I'm sure Ms. McKinnie can alter it if necessary." Then he retrieved a solid blue dress with puffy sleeves. "This one is perfect for church. It's our newest fashion. Unfortunately, that's all the dresses we have, but our material is the finest. You should take some for her to make some of her own garments. I'd suggest this one."

The fact that it was the most expensive fabric in the store didn't escape Owen, but he knew nothing about women's clothing. He'd gone through Emma Sue's things in the shed, but they were too small for Abigail and were too worn out from the elements to be mended. "I'll take the two dresses and whatever she might need to alter them." He thought for a minute, realizing he had no clue what else women needed. Heat set fire to his skin and he paced the store, trying to figure out how to ask his next question.

"Need anything else?"

"Yes," he blurted, but then couldn't manage the rest.

"What else? Perhaps some flour? Eggs?" Mr. Graham headed to the counter with the dresses in hand.

"No, I'm good there." He took off his hat and held it to his chest. "I...I don't need anything else, but Ms. McKinnie might."

Mr. Graham folded the dresses neatly and placed them in brown paper, wrapping them neatly with twine. "What might she need?"

Owen eyed the door. Perhaps he should just leave with what he purchased before this situation got any worse.

"Ah. If it's a woman thing, my wife would be happy to help." Mr. Graham tied a bow with the twine then set the package aside and waited for Owen to answer.

Owen nodded, but had no desire to deal with Mrs. Graham and her gossiping ways. "Except I don't know what she needs. Perhaps Mrs. Graham could package a few things that Ms. McKinnie will need and I'll come back to pick everything up. That way, I'm not privy to the contents of the package."

Mr. Graham beamed at the opportunity to oversell him, but what choice did Owen have? He hadn't been married long enough to know what women needed in the way of undergarments. "I'll return in a bit. I need to do a few more things in town before heading back to the homestead."

"I'll have everything packaged and ready to go by the time you return. Don't worry about what people say. I know you're a good man, Mr. Baker. You can come in to buy whatever you need anytime. And would you like me to pass on a message to Johnson when he returns?"

"I wanted to know what the Homestead Act says about women owning land. I know they can, but what are the details? Can a widow keep land? What about unmarried folk?"

Mr. Graham pursed his lips as if he knew to keep his mouth shut. "I'll get that answer for you and when you return next week for supplies, I'll let you know what he says."

The door jingled, and Owen planted his hat on his head then escaped out the door to the bustling streets. He caught sight of the woman with the pink bonnet on the other side of a line of wagons, gossiping to the local preacher. That was Owen's cue to make a run for it. He rushed down the street to the doctor's place and knocked.

"Come in," a man's voice called.

Owen entered a small room occupied only by a chair, a desk, and a curtain that separated the space from the exam room.

A man with grey hair and spectacles stood with a raise of a brow. "What can I help you with, sir?"

With his hat in hand, Owen shut the door and scanned the room for others.

"No need to be concerned. We're the only ones here. Do you have sores, son?" The old man reached into a medicine bag and pulled out a glass bottle.

"I'm sorry?"

The man eyed Owen below the belt. "Down there? You here for blisters?"

Heat galloped up his neck. "I'm not here for me."

The doctor chuckled. "Ah, you've got a wife at home. Okay, does your friend have blisters?"

Irritation nipped at Owen. "No blisters involved. Perhaps I came to the wrong place." He reached for the door and plopped his hat back on his head.

"Settle down. Why don't you sit and we can chat about what's bothering you." The man clapped him on the back. "I'm sorry for the assumption, but there's been an outbreak of genital blisters in town."

Owen didn't want to know anymore. He'd heard about these kinds of things from men on the trail who had been with women who sold themselves for money. "I assure you, sir, this is nothing in relation to a physical disease. I was hoping to speak to you about another matter, since I understand you have experience helping survivors from the war."

That sparked the doctor's interest and the drawn look on his face was replaced by enthusiasm. "Yes, son. Please sit down," he said with a sorrowful tone.

Owen sat in the only available chair as the doctor leaned against the desk. "Tell me, do you suffer nightmares? Are you prone to anger or uncontrollable crying?"

"No, it's not me. As I said, it's about a friend. She's frightened of lightning and—"

"She?" The doctor quirked a brow.

"Yes, I don't know if women can suffer the same mental ailments as men who've fought, but I do know of others who would scream out in the night on the wagon train. If a woman suffered in war the way a man did, isn't it possible she could also suffer from a similar ailment?"

The doctor tapped the table several times before he answered. "I have never heard of such a matter, but I do see how this could be possible. How fascinating."

Owen didn't find anything about Abigail's fear fascinating. The sound of her cries had broken his heart in two. Of course, that was his biggest fault. Willy had called it his damsel-in-distress syndrome, something Willy said started way before his wife died. Could it have been when he couldn't save his little sister? Owen shook off the thoughts and focused. "Is there treatment? Something I can do to help?"

He retrieved a book from a shelf and skimmed through it. "There are new studies about men having fits of madness, claiming they are still at war. The mind is confused and clouded, and from the information I've read…yes, here. *It is believed that a man relives his most horrific and tragic moments. Not as in a dream, but as if reliving it that moment. This provokes fits of terror and madness.*"

"Relives? So, she's actually reliving the terror of the soldiers?" Owen's gut twisted at the thought of Abigail being tortured over and over again by her memories of the war. He'd always carried the guilt of not fighting, but he refused to choose a side, to choose between his brothers. Maybe if he had, they would've survived. "It should be me who suffers, not a woman."

"Do you feel guilty for surviving the war? That's fairly common."

"No, it's worse. I feel guilty for not fighting."

The door to the office flew open and Owen bolted from his chair.

"Doc, we need you. Indians set fire to the mill. Several men were burned."

The doctor grabbed his bag and headed for the door before he recalled Owen. "The best medicine is time and a calm environment. Try to keep her from suffering anymore and she will hopefully get better."

"Thanks, doctor." Owen followed him out of the office and into a frenzy of men with guns mounting horses and shouting.

"Men said the Indians split up," the man told the doctor. "Most headed west, but a few headed north."

"North?" Owen asked the man. "That's where my homestead is."

"You best gather a posse and head that way, and quick. If there's anything left by the time you get there. Indians won't stop till they burn everything to the ground and murder everyone. Women and children included."

Women? "Abigail." He didn't wait for a posse. He raced to his horse, where Mr. Graham waited with his packages.

"I've put this on your account."

Owen nodded then tossed the finely wrapped merchandise onto the seat and hopped up onto the buckboard. He tore through the city and out onto the open plains. He knew her living on the prairie had been a mistake. *Not this time*, he pleaded. He wouldn't let her die.

Chapter Eight

Abigail watered the tiny lettuce sprouts peeking out of the ground. Hopefully they would have some more vegetables soon. Hearing a strange drumming sound, she abandoned her work and made her way up the hill, but saw nothing in the distance. She returned to water more of the sprouting vegetables and to pull the weeds that threatened to choke them. The low deep beat continued. After another hour, her nerves were beating at the same cadence as the distant drums. Fear and curiosity bubbled up inside her. Was this the Indian drums she'd read about? Were they going to attack with tomahawks in hand?

She wished Susan was still there. Abigail didn't even know how to find the Dunsts' homestead.

The drum beat quickened and fear dominated curiosity. She gripped the rope on the water bucket too tight, causing the pain in her hands to intensifying.

Bum. Boom. Boom. Bum. The sound of the drum pounded her skull until her head ached. She decided to load the rifle and set it by her side while she wrote to her sisters. Even in the dugout, though, she was exposed with no door.

Her hands trembled, making her penmanship look child-like, but she ignored her apprehension and continued to write. After her episode last night, she feared she'd given Owen enough fuel to argue his point that she wasn't strong enough to stay. A little pounding noise wouldn't send her into another fit of hysteria. As it was, she worried Owen had gone into town to arrange transportation to send her home. Well, when he returned, she'd refuse to leave again. If Susan was right, Owen wouldn't really tie her to a horse and force her to leave, despite all of his threats.

She had to prove she possessed a strength greater than those who had died. Perhaps someday he'd even warm up to her. The way he had last night. He'd whispered in her ear how he wouldn't leave her side, that he wouldn't abandoned her. They were only words, though, empty promises to steady her emotions. If she admitted the truth to herself, she enjoyed the way his arms wrapped around her protectively.

She shook off the thoughts and dipped her pen back into ink. She wrote to each of her sisters individually, saving the most important for last. Cora.

Dear sister,

I long to see your smiling face, but I'm afraid I'm still working to secure a home for us here in the wild prairies of Kansas. In a previous letter, I wrote of a man who ordered me off our land, but that I'd refused. A harsh man with stern ways, but since that day I've seen another side of him. He is also a gentleman with compassion and the potential for greatness.

Last night, I had an episode and to my surprise, he didn't reprimand me, or tell me how I was weak and that I needed to return home. Instead, he cared for me and kept me safe. Perhaps not all men are worthless and care only for fighting. Owen tends to his land, and speaks of his desire not to fight with his fellow man. He even abstained from fighting in the war, citing his love of his brothers over his will to fight. I assure you, he is no coward, but a man of wisdom and honor.

I confess, even with his limited company I find prairie life isolating and long for you to join me here. Most days I speak to myself, just to hear a voice. I'm pleased to share that I met our nearest neighbor, a kind woman with a sisterly way about her. It stirred my heart to work faster so that I may bring you all here soon.

Today, though, I wish for silence as the beat of an Indian drum sounds in the distance. I sit contemplating abandoning my new home and walking to town before they attack, but then I breathe the way you used to remind me to when I was stressed, and I decided if the land won't beat me, neither will Indians.

The thought of your arduous journey here causes me distress, but I know you must endure to find the happiness of home once more. I hope to send these letters to you soon, and to also write with the instructions and money for you and our sisters to head west. Together, I know we will conquer all that threatens us. The way we managed to battle our way through the war.

The drum beat sounds louder now. I confess my stress is increasing and I find myself for the first time in years wishing for a man to be near to protect me. Not that I need one. I will face whatever threatens me and I will prevail.

I only hope that you and our sisters are surviving the plague of loss and you are still finding favor with our neighbors for food in exchange for mending and working. It troubles me that you are no longer able to be served and instead must now serve others. Our old way of life is now lost forever.

The drums have stopped. I had wished the noise to cease, but now the silence is like the quiet before cannon fire upon our men at the mountain. I peeked out the door and discovered strange, oddly dressed men in the distance. If this is my last letter to you, know that I would do it all again to give you and our sisters a chance at a better life. For now, I am going to abandon my home and hide in the fields with the rifle at my side. I have and always will love you all.

Your sister,

Abigail

After folding the letter, she stood and lifted the curtain from the doorway just enough to peer outside. The men with feathers and bare chests were now congregating at the edge of the hill. They pointed to the dugout, then the line of Indians advanced. She grabbed the rifle and skirted along the side of the dugout, managing to stay hidden long enough to run for the prairie grass. She didn't dare look behind her, not when the call of an Indian sounded. Not when the sound of galloping horses echoed. Not when an arrow whooshed by her head.

In the middle of the field, she prostrated herself against the ground and prayed that the tall grass would keep her hidden. For hours, she remained frozen, listening while the Indians pillaged the dugout and rummaged through their belongings, freed their chickens and animals, and burned the barn. As the sun lowered in the sky, she longed for the darkness yet dreaded it at the same time.

The soft shuffle of footsteps approached. One Indian? She listened, pressing her ear to the earth. Her eldest brother had taught her to hunt and track when they were younger. No, two Indians had entered the field. Terror filled her and all she could do was pray. *Holy Father, please give me strength to face what comes. Protect me from thine enemy. Let me feel your presence so I may remain sane.* She closed her eyes as the sound of crunching grass drew closer.

Strange words were mumbled. The smell of ash and burned wood filled the air, reminding her of the war. The threat of men and their selfish intentions once more plagued her, yet this was much scarier than the war. During the war, she knew what the men had come for, knew their intensions. These men were completely alien to her.

She pressed her face to the earth, tasting dirt, grass, and salty tears. Gripping the gun, she braced herself for a fight. One thing she knew, they weren't taking her alive.

Chapter Nine

The buckboard bounced and the stack of wood in the back banged louder than his pulse in his ears. He should've disconnected his horse from the wagon, the added weight was only slowing him down. But he'd been in such a hurry he didn't even think of it. His mind reeled with images of the Indians scalping and killing Abigail. He urged the horse to gallop faster, the wheels of the wagon nearly taking flight, threatening to overturn.

The smell of smoke invaded his lungs. Was it the smoke from the mill? No, the wind was blowing from the direction of the homestead. He crested the hill and saw smoke billowing on the horizon. A sting of terror shot through him, slicing his heart into shreds. "Abigail." Not caring that the clatter of the wheels and the kicked-up cloud of dust would announce his arrival, he continued to drive the horse faster and harder.

As he drew closer, he saw them. Indians, some on horseback, others by the dugout, more in the field. No sign of Abigail. He continued to scan the area, but saw nothing. The Indians at the dugout spotted him and hollered a battle cry, wrenching the evening silence. Seven of them and only one sidearm to defend himself with. Still, he didn't stop.

Then red popped up above the sea of brown grass—Abigail's hair flowing like a wild mane. As he watched, she slowly rose with the rifle pointed at two Indians only a few paces from her. He let go of the reins with one hand and drew his hand gun with the other. The Indians at the dugout advanced on him while the others scattered into the field.

She fired the rifle. It kicked, sending her back a few paces. One Indian fell to the ground, while the other lunged at her. Owen pulled the horse to a halt and fired two shots.

The Indians on horseback raced toward him, quickly closing the distance when another shot was fired, this time from the top of the hill. Owen looked up to see Martin with his own rifle. Abigail fired another shot and Owen followed suit. The

Indians scattered through the prairie grass toward the creek, carrying their injured with them.

Owen jumped from the buckboard and raced to Abigail. She turned the gun on him with fire in her eyes. He dropped his handgun to the ground and held his hands up, shuffling closer to her. "It's me. Owen. I won't hurt you."

The rifle bounced in her shaking hands as her eyes scanned wildly about before she took a stuttered breath, nodded, and lowered the gun. He unfurled her fingers from the gunstock and retrieved the gun from her bleeding hands. "It's over."

Abigail stumbled forward, but instead of falling into his arms, she lifted her head high and walked past him to the dugout and disappeared inside. Martin met him outside the dugout. "She okay? Susan told me she was here alone. When I heard the drums, I rode as fast as I could."

Owen's head spun with thoughts of Abigail being harmed. "Thank you. I owe you one," he said, his voice shaking.

Martin slapped him on the back. "You owe me nothing. We're neighbors, remember?"

Owen clutched his arm and squeezed in gratitude since the words had gotten stuck in his throat with emotion. "She could've—"

"She's fine. A little shaken up for sure, but the way she held that rifle, I'd say she can handle herself. Even on the prairie."

"I'm taking her to town. She shouldn't be here." Owen moved for the dugout, but Martin cut him off.

"Do you know what's waiting for her back home? Did you ever think that maybe this is less dangerous than where you'd be sending her back to?"

Owen fisted his hands. "It can't be worse."

"It can. Trust me." Martin released him. "That woman needs someone to sooth her right now, not send her away. She's had enough stress for one day."

Stress. The doctor had warned him she should avoid it. He took in a long, smoke-filled breath, needing a second, and assessed the carnage of his barn. If she screamed in terror at thunder, who knew what kind of state she'd be in after the Indians? He gave way to Martin's reasoning. "I best get in there and check on her. Thanks again."

Martin nodded and hurried back to his horse which he'd left tied to a tree on the hillside. Owen swallowed hard and took a minute to compose himself before he entered the dugout. Abigail needed a strong man who could help her through this, not one who scolded her to leave.

He found Abigail scurrying about, wiping the table down, straightening letters she'd written, making the bed. Not the crying, hysterical woman hiding in the corner he'd expected.

"Abigail, are you well?" He nudged toward her but she scooted away and stacked dishes on the edge of the table.

"Fine. I told you I could handle myself, so you can stop trying to send me away." Her voice trembled.

"You should sit down." Owen pulled out a chair.

She threw the dirty, musty rag at him, and it plastered to his chest. He peeled it away and set it on the table. "I'm not going to let you toss me in the wagon and take me into town, so stop trying to make me feel like I can't handle this place. I can." Abigail paced around the small room, waving her arms about. "You work your land, I'll work mine, and we'll be fine. I don't need your help. I don't need anyone's help," she screeched, her voice hitching an octave higher.

"Calm down. I'm not going to force you to leave," Owen said.

She continued pacing. "I'll handle Indians, gunmen, storms, whatever the prairie throws at me, and I won't need you to save me."

Owen grabbed her arms and forced her to stop. She struggled, her eyes wild, hair falling over her beautiful face. "Stop. Just stop. Everyone needs somebody."

She yanked her arm, but he wouldn't let go. "You don't. Remember? You're tough, you don't need or want anyone. Well, I'm just as tough, so get out of my way. I have work to do."

"You're not going back out there. Not right now." She pushed and clawed at him to release her, but he couldn't let her go running out into the field in a fit, not with Indians still out there. "Calm down."

She wrenched free and slapped him across the face, leaving the sting of her hand on his cheek. She gasped and stumbled back. "I'm sorry. I didn't mean to…but you wouldn't let me go."

He cornered her against the wall, slow and calm. "Everyone needs somebody. Right now, I need you."

Her lip trembled, her chest rose and fell with exaggerated breaths. The curtain flapped at the doorway and she glanced over at it then back at him. She was intense and beautiful, delicate yet strong. He touched her fingers, lightly grazing her to keep her calm. “We need to build a door tonight. With Indians out there, we can’t be exposed like this any longer.” He brushed the stray hair from her face so he could see the deep green of her eyes. “If you’re gonna stay, I want it to be as safe as possible.” He didn’t mean for her to stay forever, just until he could establish a place for her in the city. If Martin was right, and Georgia was worse than here, then he’d find her a respectable husband or job in Prairie City where she’d be safe.

“It’s not a trick? You won’t tie me to the buckboard and force me to leave?” Abigail breathed more than spoke, her tone raspy and inviting.

“No, you’d just find a way back here even if I did.”

She chuckled. “I’m glad you understand that now.” Her hands still trembled and her lip quivered. He wanted to pull her into his arms and hold her until morning, the way he did the night before. Abigail touched his cheek where she’d smacked him, but instead of calming him, it only proved to stoke the fire within him more. “I’m sorry about that. I thought you were going to force me to leave.” She stood on her tiptoes and pressed her lips to his cheek, stealing his breath and heart, but not his resolve. It only fueled his desire to get her far away from the homestead, and even further away from him before something terrible happened, like he fell in love with her.

With the door finally hung and the wooden security bar in place, they both relaxed at the table for a cup of coffee and conversation. Abigail handed a tin cup to Owen then sat by his side. "You're great at building things. The windmills are amazing, and you can build a door in an evening."

"Yes, and you can catch chickens in near darkness. And fix the wire so they can't escape again. That's what I'd call talented." Owen lifted his cup as if to toast their accomplishments.

She sipped the lukewarm, bitter drink and sighed. "I'm afraid the barn is ruined, but the animals are safe, though they're scattered."

The wind stirred outside and Owen eyed her as if the smallest sound would startle her.

"I'm fine. I promise not to freak out if there's a little rain." She ran her finger around the rim of the cup. “I never got to formally apologize or thank you for helping me last night.”

He held his cup in mid-air for a moment as if contemplating his words carefully. “No need to thank me. We all have our…challenges with our pasts.”

She set her cup down and placed her hand over his knuckles. “I know you’ve suffered, too.”

“I didn’t fight in the war.” He shrugged out of her touch, and she wilted back into her chair.

“We all have our battles to fight. There’s no shame in not fighting.” She shook her head. “Looking back, it was so stupid. The call to defend the honor of our Southern ways. Our men ready to fight for the right to keep other men as their property and the women fawning over their bravery. I was one of those girls. My fiancé went off to war and died within a month. My eldest brother fought on the frontlines and died. My second brother died in a train crash on the way to fight near Marietta. That’s when my mother fell ill. Within a month, she died. Then my father died shortly after of a broken heart.” She swallowed, trying to clear the lump from her throat. “And then my little brother, too young to fight in a man’s war, tried to save my sister from ruin by a Union soldier when the war came to our doorstep." Her voice cracked and tears filled her eyes, blurring her vision. Owen scooted his chair closer, to where their knees nearly touched. "He couldn't save her though, and died at the hands of the enemy."

Owen took her hands in his and squeezed tight. "You've lost so many. I had no idea."

She sniffled and swallowed back the horrific memories. "We all lose people. It's part of life. It doesn't matter if you live in mansions near the city with fine dresses, or wear trousers and live on a farm."

"When did you speak with Mrs. Dunst?" Owen shifted, the chair creaking under his weight.

His sorrow-filled gaze locked with hers and she found it hard to breathe. They were so close, closer than she'd been to any man emotionally before. "Earlier today."

"It wasn't her place to tell you those things," he said.

The man wasn't all rugged farmer after all. She was pleased with their new agreement, but she still didn't believe he was fully committed to letting her stay.

His shoulders slumped. "I know you're trying to convince me that you should stay. Perhaps you should…in time. There are fine hotels in Prairie City. Once more homesteaders move here, and the Indians are under control—"

"Then what? Fever could take me, an infection, a fall. You can't hide from death. It'll find you whether you like it or not. Trust me. I've seen it up close."

"Yes, but why take the extra risk? There are women who live in Prairie City and make dresses to support themselves, and there are respectable jobs at the general stores and other businesses."

"I get what you're doing, but it's not going to work. I'm staying on my land."

Owen sighed then let go of her hands and stood. "Then I guess it's time I gave you something. No sense in you suffering more than you have to living out here." He opened the front door and disappeared for a minute before returning with wrapped packages tied with twine. "These are for you. I…um…don't know what's in one of them. I asked Mrs. Graham from the general store to pack some woman things. The other two I picked out though. I hope you like them." His face tinted pink, and his gaze traveled to the floor.

It had been years since anyone had given her anything. Lately, men had only taken from her family. Emotion stirred, tightening her chest. "What is it?"

"Open it and you'll find out." Owen returned to his coffee.

She unwrapped the first package and discovered a dress far more practical than the one she'd traveled in, but still pretty. "Thank you. It's lovely. You didn't have to do that, though."

Owen rubbed the back of his neck. "I know, but you need something proper to wear or people will talk. They're already whispering about the fact we both live out here together."

Abigail rolled her eyes. "Let them talk. Funny how that once bothered me so much, but when you face real issues, harmful words no longer hold power." She couldn't believe she once allowed what other people thought to rule her every decision.

"Open that one, too." He pointed at the thick package with a boyish smile.

She ripped into it. The sight of the beautiful, blue dress took her breath away. "Oh, Owen, you shouldn't have. This must've cost a fortune. I promise I'll pay you back."

Owen's mouth fell open in a wounded *O* shape. "It's a gift."

She launched into him and kissed his cheek. “It’s the most beautiful gift. Thank you.”

The room fell silent. No howl of a wild dog, no Indian drum beat, not even the wind could be heard. Her breath caught at the contact. It was simply a thank you kiss, but it surged heat through her body. She slid against him until her feet were flat on the ground once more, and she shied away from him. A surge of excitement took hold of her. Judging by the redness on his face, he felt it, too. Nerves drove her to unladylike fidgeting, something that would’ve driven her mother crazy. Still, she couldn’t stop her hands from playing with the hem of the dress.

He cleared his throat and took a swig of coffee. “I’m glad you like it. I’ve never chosen a dress before. Mr. Graham said you could alter it to fit. The supplies to do so are in the other package. As I said, I’m not sure what’s in there.” He stood, knocking into the table and sloshing dark liquid onto the wood. “I, um, should let you get some rest if you want to go to visit with the Dunsts tomorrow.” He snagged the cup, dipped it in the bucket of water beside the wood stove and hung it on a nail to dry. “I’ll get to work on repairing the barn in the morning, and it looked like the roof of the outhouse was scorched from some embers that flew over."

His prattling on made her smile. She usually had to force full sentences out of him and now he was chattering on like a schoolboy. "I'll help with the rebuild. If we work together, we can finish early and have more time for a visit."

He nodded without even a word of argument about her not using her hands until they were fully healed. "I'll see you in the morning."

"Wait," she said. "The Indians. You can't stay outside tonight. That's why you built the door, remember? To protect us in the night."

He straightened to his full, impressive height and snagged his hat from the nail at the side of the door. "It's not proper for us to stay in here together. People will talk."

Abigail shuffled closer, but he backed away, his hand on the door ready to escape. "I told you I don't care what people think. I care about safety."

"All the same, I'll sleep outside at night. Unless it storms. Then I'll sleep in the shed."

"Don't be absurd. There isn't room in the shed. You'd have to pull out all the supplies to fit in there." She moved closer, but he pressed himself against the door as if she'd set him on fire with her touch.

"Goodnight, ma'am." He placed his hat on his head, wrenched the door open, slipped outside and shut it behind him, closing off any further discussion.

The thought of him out there all night made her heart ache with worry. She knew there'd be no convincing him otherwise, not tonight, so she settled on top of the bed with the blue dress held tight to her chest. Men used to shower her with gifts to impress her, woo her, and win her affection. But this was different. This was a gift from his heart.

Curiosity drew her to the last package. She opened it to find a chemise and womanly unmentionables. The image of him asking for woman's undergarments nearly made her fall off the bed laughing. The once rude, self-absorbed man with an attitude had softened, if only a little. Yet, she knew he still wanted to send her away. The thought of leaving the homestead, of leaving Owen's company, weighed her down with sorrow.

She closed her eyes, realizing she needed to focus on her sisters, not on the man who plotted to corrupt her resolve with kindness. Her sisters had and always would come first, and tomorrow morning she'd tell him it was time to send for her sisters. She'd manage to build a larger home and secure it before they could arrive. They'd have more people to work and protect their land from Indians. After all, they could fight Indians, they couldn't fight starvation. No more waiting. Together with her sisters, she knew they could all make this a real home. A home with everyone she loved and cherished. For the first time in years, hope wasn't just a word to Abigail. It meant everything.

Owen eyed the horizon, looking for any signs of storms or Indians. To his relief, the skies looked bright and happy, like his mood. Despite the burned barn and having to fix the fencing, his feet were light. For the first time in months, he didn't feel the dark cloud of loss shadowing him.

Abigail worked hard, helping to frame the new, larger barn and gathering supplies for the thatch roofing. He had to admit, though, he wished she would've worn her new dress. Although she did wear the sun bonnet he'd gotten for her. The only regret was that it covered her beautiful hair and eyes. He'd never seen such a vivid color of hair before. Nothing on earth even matched the depth and brilliance of it.

With the afternoon sun beating down on him, he decided it was a great time to take a break. "You ready to head out to the Dunst place? We should go before it gets too late. I don't want to be near the woods after dark."

She dropped her bundle of thatching and wiped her hands on the apron she wore, an item Mrs. Graham must've included for her. He wondered what other items had been sent, but shook off the inappropriate thoughts. Abigail wasn't like the saloon girls with their overt sexuality, or fragile like Emma Sue had been. No, Abigail possessed strength beyond any woman he'd ever met, yet she was delicate in the way she carried herself. He hated the blisters that marred her soft hands, but he enjoyed working side by side with her, even more than he had Willy.

"Sure, but I need a minute to freshen up. Do you mind if I bathe at the creek? I'd like to wear appropriate attire, but I don't want to put on one of my new dresses in this state." She showed him her dirtied hands and arms.

He eyed the horizon. The creek was too far to protect her if the Indians returned. "Only if I go with you." That darn heat flooded his face once more and he felt like a schoolboy trying to ask to carry a girl's books for her. "I mean, I won't watch." He removed his hat and swiped the sweat pooling around his hairline. “I’ll be on the other side of the creek, watching the distant woods for any sign of Indians. I’ll have my back to you the entire time.”

Abigail nodded then smiled and hip-bumped him. “Imagine what the townspeople will say when they hear you were with me when I bathed.” She sauntered past with a sway of her hips he hadn’t expected, a flirtatious, almost shocking walk.

“Not funny. Your reputation would be ruined.”

“Oh, the scandal.” She waved her hand in front of her face like a fan before opening the door and retrieving the package from the bed. “I’ve already told you that I don’t care what people think. I only care about making this homestead work and providing what I need. I’ll not be run out of town because of what people think.” The brown paper crinkled in her arms. She stopped by his side and winked at him. “Coming?"

He grabbed the rifle and followed a few steps behind, attempting to get his imagination under control. He would not let this woman draw him in to the point where he felt the need to marry her and save her from herself. He’d already tried that route and failed miserably. But if Abigail remained unmarried, he suspected she couldn’t own land, which meant she'd lose everything she worked so hard for. Even if he didn't want to marry, or have anyone around, it was wrong that she couldn't own her own land just because she was an unmarried woman. She worked as hard as any other homesteader he'd met.

She reached the top of the hill, passed the windmill and stopped at the edge of the widest part of the creek without even a glance around to ensure the area was safe.

The darkness threatened to return at the sight of the graves on the hill near the large oak tree.

Water rippled over rocks and birds chirped nearby, but she said nothing. She placed the brown package near the creek and approached him. "Yes, I've been here before. I know about your wife and the child you lost." Her fingers whispered over his, a slight touch that could move mountains. "I'm sorry for your loss. But if I've learned anything from the war, it's that you can't live in the past. Sometimes you must look ahead, even when you think there's no way to go on with life." Her voice cracked, and he threaded his fingers through hers, squeezing in an attempt to comfort her.

"I do look forward. That's why I didn't want you here. It's tough and rugged and dangerous.

Take yesterday. If I'd been a few minutes later…" His gut clenched so tight he couldn't breathe.

"It's not your job to protect me. I don't want a man to take care of me. I want to take care of myself, and my family back in Georgia. You worry that I want you to marry me to save me from life, but I don't. I'm not like your wife. I don't need a man to save me."

He released her hands, the connection too powerful for him to think. What was happening? He'd never felt these kinds of stirrings with his late wife, or any other woman. "What if you couldn't work your land? Then what would you do?"

Distant rustling in the woods drew his attention, and he gripped the rifle tight in his hand.

"It's just an animal. There're no drums today. I think we're safe for now." She sauntered passed him and gave a coy smile over her shoulder. "No one is taking my land away. It won't happen. But the scandal will have merit if you don't turn around soon." She untied the apron and he couldn't look away, not for several seconds. It was as if his body had taken over his brain.

The rustling in the woods broke his trance and he carried his rifle to the other side of the creek to stand guard facing the woods. At the first splash of water, he thought he'd lose control and turn around. The thought of her perfect frame completely visible in the daylight stirred him. It had been a long time since he'd felt a woman under him. Yet, he knew these moments of attraction were no more than his baser needs demanding attention.

What was he doing? This woman had stumbled onto his homestead, into his life, and into his dreams. Now, he didn't know what to do. Did he want them to take her land? That would make her return to Georgia. Or did he want her to succeed and stay here, for no other reason than having a work partner he could get along with? He told himself he didn't want anything else from her. He'd build her a house nearby and the distance between them would help cool his desires.

After several painstaking minutes, she began to sing while she bathed, a soft, foreign-sounding tune. "What's that?" he asked.

"An Irish folk song my mother used to sing."

He needed to keep his mind off the fact she was naked and only a few feet away. "What's it about?"

"It's a tale about two forbidden lovers lost in the mist. One is a princess from a magical realm who loves her people. The other is a farmer who must protect his land by killing all things unnatural in the woods. According to legend, the princess is the most physically-enchanting beauty, with hair of fire-gold. He is a strong and honorable man. She is charged with finding a new place for her people to live before they are cast from the living forever."

More splashes and then a small sigh carried from the creek bed to his ears.

"What happened?" he asked, more to keep his mind on something other than Abigail.

"One night, he hears her whispers on the wind. So, he travels through the mist to the top of a hill and discovers her standing, looking over his land. With one look at him, she falls deeply and madly in love, forgetting about her people. Believing her human, he doesn't kill her, so she follows him into the world between the mist and his land. For many moons they join in a forbidden romance, until a farmer from his town stumbles into the mist and discovers them."

"So, the farmer tells the people in the mist?" he asks.

She giggled then water dripping in loud droplets sounded before he heard her soft steps from the creek onto the land. He swallowed hard and kept his eyes trained on the woods. "No, his people order a raid into the mist and many mortals died. The princess is now cursed because of her failure to find a new home for her people and is forever trapped in her madness." The brown paper crinkled, so he knew she would be dressed soon. He said a silent prayer of thanks that he hadn't completely lost his mind, jumped over the creek and took her in his arms in the middle of the prairie.

"And the farmer?"

"He is hanged from a rope at the edge of the mist for his crimes. She races to save him, but is trapped in the mist only a few steps from saving him for all eternity. They are cursed to remain steps apart and relive their failure to save each other as her people wither away into the dirt."

"That's a haunting song. Are all Irish tales so depressing?"

She laughed. "Many are, but it's a tale that is told each time there is a bad crop. They say her people are cursing the mortals who tricked their princess from saving them."

"Does the legend say it can follow an Irish woman to a new land?" he teased.

"I think you're safe. And you can turn around now."

He took a long breath of relief knowing she now wore clothes, but when he turned his desire only burned hotter. The simple print dress flowed from her hips, fit snug at her waist and chest, but the sleeves were a bit long. Her red hair fell freely down her back. Damp from the creek, it glistened in the sun.

"What's wrong? Does the dress not flatter me?"

He hopped the creak and stood a breath from her. His hands shook with the desire to pull her against him, but he fought it. "No, it's the opposite. You look perfect."

She dipped her chin toward her chest then shyly glanced at him. "Thank you."

He set the gun down against a tree and returned to her side. When she straightened after wrapping her package, there was no space between them. Chest-to-chest, they eyed each other, the brown package the only thing stopping him from touching her. Her eyes burned with desire, and he knew at that moment she longed to kiss him. And there was nothing more in the world he wanted than to feel her lips on his.

He cradled her neck with his hand and dared to edge her lips closer to his. Her gaze darted about from his eyes to his lips, yet she melted into him only to tense. "We should get going before it's too late."

Abigail's words hung in the air like a rejection. He backed away, cursing himself for advancing on her. The woman he'd been trying to persuade to leave, a woman he'd never marry, or even wanted on the homestead.

"Owen. I—"

"You're right. We should go." He moved away, but she grabbed his arm.

"Owen."

"No need. I'm—"

"Look," she squealed.

He turned to find an Indian woman and child standing on the other side of the creek, watching them.

Chapter Twelve

The Indian woman, dressed in animal skins with a young boy at her side, stood perfectly still with no indication of movement. Owen reached for his rifle, but Abigail wouldn't let him go from her grip.

"No, don't."

"What?" His eyebrows rose high on his face and his muscles tensed at her demand.

"Trust me." Abigail could see something in the woman's eyes, something only another woman would see. She was almost positive this Indian didn't come for a fight. She probably came for peace, to end the men's war. Abigail moved toward the creek, but Owen stopped her.

"That's far enough."

"She's not here to harm us." She shrugged away from him and moved to the edge of the creek.

The Indian across from her did the same. Abigail's heart thundered, beating against her chest faster than those Indian drums from the day before.

The woman remained on the other side of the embankment, but knelt at the thinnest part of the creek and wiped at the dirt in front of her. The woman with her son gestured for Abigail to do the same. "Sit," he said in a strange accent. "Not hurt."

She'd heard tales while on the train about Indians learning white man's tongue and even trading furs and such with settlers. Abigail hiked up her dress and sat on her knees, mimicking the woman in front of her. She didn't have to look behind her to feel the tension coming from Owen.

The woman drew strange figures in the dirt, ones Abigail recognized as men, guns, and buffalo, but she wasn't sure what the woman was trying to tell her. She hoped she'd be able to understand the woman's message, and stop the violence before another war broke out and her lands were burned and destroyed.

The drawing continued and she could hear Owen behind her shifting between feet, breathing rapidly and shallow. She prayed he wouldn't panic and shoot them. If she'd grown to know Owen the way she thought she had, he wasn't an impulsive man prone to violence. He was different than most, something that kept drawing her to the man despite her desire to keep a distance.

The woman stopped drawing and sat back. Abigail eyed the figures in the dirt and tried to make sense of it.

Owen squatted by her side. "That is the move of the Indians by our troops, forcing them to leave their homes," he said, his voice low and disturbed. "I hadn't realized how us moving out west was driving them from their lands. The Indians have always been savage, killing with no remorse. At least according to the reports. They set fire to the mill only yesterday, and think about our barn and the threat they made to you."

Abigail noticed the homestead was drawn and a wheel she assumed represented the mill. "I think her men probably did that to show force, to show that they should not be taken lightly and that we should stop settling on their lands."

"Sacred lands of my people. White man ruin," the boy said in a tone of hatred. The woman said something in their language and the boy bowed his head. "Wish to live without white men take everything. Tried free animals."

Abigail's heart wrenched at the realization. Their land, the homestead she swore she wouldn't lose to any man, had never been hers to begin with. The Indians had been here long before the settlers came. "That's why they burned the barn. They wanted the animals free," she mumbled. "I'm sorry about your land. I didn't know."

Owen patted her knee. "We didn't know." He sighed. "Those men in town took their setting fire to the mill as an act of war. They won't stop until they've killed all of the Indians responsible."

The wind picked up and a chill went through her. "And if they kill the Indians, what do you think the Indians will do? They'll retaliate, and man's war will never end."

Water continued to trickle over the smooth rocks of the creek bed while they all sat staring at one another. "We will speak to the town," Abigail offered finally. "If you do not attack us anymore, perhaps I can convince them not to kill anyone else."

The boy shook his head. "Too many words. Don't know."

Abigail swiped her hand on the dirt and drew with her finger the mill, the men, guns, and the Indians. When she was done, she placed an *X* over the drawing of the fire to the mill and to her homestead. She looked up to see the woman analyzing her drawing. Then she put an *X* over the image of horses and guns chasing the Indians. Her drawing was crude, and she only hoped the woman understood.

They sat in silence for a moment, the weight of their conversation heavy in the air. Then the Indian woman spoke to the boy and he nodded. Looking at Owen and Abigail, he said, "Our people not attack, your people not attack."

She didn't know how to explain she couldn't make that promise, so she only nodded and vowed to do everything in her power to make it true.

Owen relaxed at her side as if the realization of the Indians' purpose was finally setting in, but then Abigail saw the truth in the Indian woman's eyes. She too couldn't guarantee her men's actions. The only hope was that the women could make the men see the usefulness of a treaty. But men were always prone to violence and war.

The Indian woman rose along with her son. Abigail followed and then Owen. The woman said something Abigail didn't understand, but she assumed it was equivalent to wishing her good luck. Then the woman and her son disappeared into the woods, leaving Owen and Abigail with a more difficult job than farming a homestead. They had to convince a town full of scared white men not to murder anymore savages who they believed would scalp them in the night.

Chapter Thirteen

For four days, Owen thought about how to convince the townspeople to not attack the Indians in retaliation for burning the mill. Men were already searching for where the Indians were living on the other side of the creek, but so far they hadn't found them.

Martin lifted the wood beam up to Owen, who settled it in as the main support beam of his new home. The man worked as hard as Abigail. He was a good, noble man with a strong back and strong morals. "What do you think you'll say to the townspeople?" Martin asked. "There's a lot of fear when it comes to Indians 'round these parts. Do you think they'll listen? Some of their men were injured by the latest fire at the mill."

Owen eyed the new barn he'd built with Abigail's help and remembered the terror the

Indians had brought to his land only days ago. At that moment, he would've shot all the men to make sure Abigail stayed safe. "Don't know yet. I'm going to think on it until Sunday. Church seems like a good place to bring it up. No one'll lynch me with a preacher there," Owen half joked. The heat of the sun continued to beat down, but a hint of gold on a nearby tree warned that fall was coming soon. They needed to get this house done in the next few months if they were going to survive winter. Not to mention stocking up on salted meats and supplies.

"Sounds like a solid plan." Martin climbed down the ladder and drank some water. "What about Abigail? You two look comfortable with each other. More comfortable than I've seen you be with most."

Owen scratched the back of his neck, but the itch didn't go away. It had settled there ever since he started to think more about Abigail being a permanent resident. "Even if I thought she could handle living on the prairie, which I'm still concerned about, she might not be able to keep her land."

Martin lined another board up to finish framing the outer wall. "What do you mean?"

"Remember me telling you about how I decided to settle here. When Emma and I stopped because Thomas had fallen ill, her father started talking about homesteading here. I'd spent enough time with them on the trail to know her father to be a drunk. I knew he'd never be able to manage the land, and the last of her money would be wasted. They couldn't travel any longer with Thomas being ill, and according to the Homesteading Act an unmarried woman couldn't own land. Not if she was widowed before buying property."

"That's why you married her. I always wondered. I could tell there wasn't any deep love between you two. Not like a husband and wife."

Owen shrugged. "It never reached the husband and wife stage. The night we married she came down with the fever. A week later, I buried her beside Thomas." Darkness crept into him the way fever managed to wiggle into the body before you even knew you were sick. "Sometimes I wonder if I did the right thing. Maybe her father could've taken better care of her."

Abigail and Susan came into sight at the edge of the homestead with baskets in hand. Wisps of her golden-red hair poking out from the bonnet shined in the sunlight.

"You've got it bad," Martin teased. "Trust me. You're gonna marry that girl."

Owen realized Martin was watching him watch Abigail. Chagrinned, he diverted his attention back to the job at hand and hammered his finger instead of the nail. After a few choice words, he shook off the pain and managed to drive the nail into the wood.

Martin shook his head and hammered in the lower part of the board. "You need to let go of your guilt and look at the future. You know Emma Sue would've been beaten and died staying in that man's custody. You did fine by her. Probably gave her a moment of happiness before she went home to the Lord. You're a good man, even if you're stubborn."

The women entered the dugout, allowing Owen's attention to fully return on the new house. He stepped back, eyeing the completed frame of the home. It made him think maybe Abigail could have a home here. She deserved to live in something besides a dugout. If she insisted on staying, she would need to have more protection than a few sticks and sod for a roof. No. The house would be for when the land was safe. Perhaps he could get her to move into town until more settlers tamed the land, and the situation with the Indians was settled with the townspeople. "It would be best if Abigail lived in town for a while. Maybe in a year or so she can move back onto her property. If she knows I'm working it for her, maybe she'll agree."

"You think she'll agree to that?" Martin quirked an eyebrow at him.

"Ahhh!" Susan screamed from inside the dugout.

Martin raced two steps ahead of Owen. They flung open the door and found Susan behind the kitchen table with her hand to her chest and Abigail with a cleaver in her hand. She slammed the blade down on the windowsill. It was only then that Owen saw the snake. The rattler had curled up in the sun.

Martin pulled Susan into his side and kissed her forehead. Owen stood there dumbfounded, eyeing Abigail as she lifted the snake, minus its head.

She analyzed the length of it and smiled. "We've got dinner."

Martin busted out laughing, a full gut kind of laugh. "You have any doubt now?"

Abigail looked between them then shrugged and put the dead snake into a pot and cleaned the cleaver.

Owen stumbled forward. Memories of fever, wagon accidents, gun shots, and death bombarded his mind. He took her hands, looking for bites on her delicate skin. "Are you insane? It could've bit you."

Abigail chuckled. "It was facing the other way when you opened the door. I took advantage and now we have supper."

Owen let her go and made his way back outside, trying to find air. His lungs constricted and he thought he'd never breathe again. The thought of that venomous serpent striking her stole the air from his lungs. Martin followed him to the water bucket and he shook his head.

"She can't stay here right now. I never seem to be able to keep people from dying. My sister died when she was six." Owen scooped water from the bucket and took a long draw, hoping the coolness would soothe his stinging lungs.

The women exited the dugout and stood outside in the sun talking.

"You never told me what happened," Martin prompted. "How old were you?"

"Fifteen." Owen wiped his mouth free of droplets and let out a loud puff of air, trying to keep the memories from consuming him. "Died in a wagon crash. It tumbled down the side of a ridge." He swallowed the gigantic lump of regrets and shame, and forced the words he'd never said aloud before. "I was tugging on the horse to get the wheels out of a rut one second…and the next…" He gasped for another gulp of air. "The next, the wagon and horses were gone."

Martin removed his hat and put it to his chest as if to mourn his loss with him. He'd proved himself time and time again to be a true friend.

"By the time we reached the bottom of the ridge she was dead, trapped under the wagon."

A long moment passed between them. Then Martin slapped him on the shoulder with brotherly force. "You were just a kid yourself. You know that wasn't your fault, right? Just like Emma Sue's and Thomas's deaths weren't. You've had it rougher than most, but you can't deny your heart. You look at Abigail the way I look at my Susan. You married the first time to save a girl. Maybe this time you marry an equal partner. She's tough and perfect for you. This time, marry for love."

Owen looked at their progress again. Building things always made him happy, but the thought of building a life with someone was far more difficult. "I can't fail someone else. I'm not strong enough."

"You're plenty strong. The problem is you try to control what happens to people. You can't do that. Even if you succeed in sending her back, Abigail could die on the train back to Georgia. Would you blame yourself then?"

Owen knew better than to say what he thought, because Martin had a point. If something happened to Abigail, even while not in his care, he'd blame himself.

Martin patted his shoulder again and placed his hat back on his head. "Only God can control things. Sorry to tell you, but you're no god."

Owen shook his head. "Nope, I'm certainly not that." His mood lighter, he smiled a little at the sight of the women walking toward them.

Abigail smiled back, revealing dark stains on her teeth. He broke out in laughter, stress-relieving, gut-busting laughter. He hadn't noticed their black mouths in the heat of the rattlesnake massacre.

Martin shot him a sideways glance, but soon joined in. "Woman, you been picking berries or eating them?" he said, slipping his arm around Susan.

Both girls bowed their heads and dabbed at their mouths. Owen brushed his thumb across Abigail's lips. She shivered under his touch and leaned into him. Martin kissed his wife. "Best berries I've ever tasted."

Suddenly, Owen wanted to taste those berries more than he needed to breathe. He could only imagine how the sweetness of the blackberries mixed with the sweetness of Abigail's lips.

The smell of fresh fruit drew him closer and his body heated with the closeness. He wiped more berry juice from the corner of her mouth. Her lips parted with a sharp exhale. Desire took hold of his mind and he pressed his lips, only a slight touch, to the corner of her mouth. She gasped, but didn't pull away. For one moment, he'd tasted the most delicious fruit he'd ever experienced in his life. His lips tingled at the contact and his breath lodged in his lungs, unable to escape, as if savoring the luscious aroma.

Susan cleared her throat.

Thankful for the interruption, he stepped back before he lost all sense and reason. He licked his lips, relishing the remnant of syrupy goodness.

A hand clapped him on his shoulder before he realized Abigail had retreated to the dugout. "You want me to drive you to the preacher now? Looks like you're headed there soon."

Owen cleared his throat, freeing it from any residue of misplaced thoughts and unwanted feelings. "Don't be ridiculous."

Martin shook his head and took Susan by the hand. "We need to be heading back to our place, but I'd be happy to take you two tomorrow if you're so inclined."

Angry clouds formed in the distance, warning of a coming storm. "Yeah, you best be going."

Martin backed away, but kept running his mouth. "You need to get to the altar before you do something that will eat your conscious up. Not to mention the townspeople are already talking about your sinful life here on the homestead."

Susan smacked him and tugged him toward their wagon.

"I'd never…" Owen protested, but the way his body craved contact with Abigail he knew that house needed to be finished soon. If not, he feared they'd both be ruined, or worse, married.

Chapter Fourteen

Abigail held tight to the post that held up the front porch Owen had built across the front of the dugout to sleep under, trying to keep her hands from touching other things. She'd never had to fight to keep her hands off her fiancé, God rest his soul. She loved him, but it had always felt like the kind of love she had for her brothers, not this belly-stirring kind of feeling. Perhaps it was the ruggedness of the terrain, the never-ending sense of danger from sun up until sun down that kept her body stirred. It didn't matter. She needed to remain focused. She needed a time frame, a goal. "I'd like to mail some letters back home."

Thunder struck and she jumped. Immediately, Owen pulled her into his side, wrapping a protective arm around her. "We can go inside. No need to stress you out here."

She shook her head. "No, it's time I face my fears."

His hand touched the middle of her back to steady her which only jolted her insides once more. "We can take your letters with us on Sunday. I spoke to Martin about the situation with the Indians. I think church would be the best place to bring up this new information. It won't be taken well by the townspeople."

The wind picked up and branches on a nearby tree bent nearly to the ground. She eyed the sky and the darkening clouds. Storms moved quickly out here. "If the Indians set fire to the mill, and hurt people, I can imagine the discord you're about to face. Fear is the kindling for a great blaze of hatred."

He quirked a half-smile at her. "I never thought of it that way." His hand moved from her back to her forearm.

Another flash of light chained across the sky and Abigail tensed, waiting for the thunder to follow.

"The open land makes storms look closer than they are," Owen said. After a few moments, the thunder rumbled. "I'd say it's still about seven miles away."

She longed to get her mind off the storm and the angry, loud thunder it would undoubtedly bring. This time she'd manage to keep her wits and not freak out. "Will someone be at the post office on Sunday?"

"Yes, but if not, we can leave the letters with Mr. Graham, the merchant. He'll mail it for you." Another roll of thunder, this time a little louder, echoed through the prairie. Owen snugged her back into his side.

Abigail fought her desire to run inside at the increased wind speed and threat of the storm.

"It's okay. I've got you," Owen whispered in her ear, his warm breath stirring her again.

"I'm fine. I won't freak out." She lifted her chin high and forced the fear from her mind.

Owen squeezed her. "Did I ever tell you about the man I knew in St. Joseph? The one who managed to escape the war after he lost his will to fight?"

"No." Abigail figured he was trying to keep her mind off the approaching storm, so she listened.

A mist on the wind began to dampen their clothes. Owen took a long breath before speaking again. "He almost killed me. Twice."

Abigail sucked in a quick breath. “What? Why?”

“He was my friend, and a good man, but the battlefront became too much for him. He’d seen too much and lived the horror. Unfortunately, the horror didn’t let him go when he was discharged. Nightmares plagued him. Anxiety made his hands shake. Loud noises in town made him tremble. Once, I startled him and he almost stabbed me.”

“Oh, my.” She mumbled.

“Shouts made him hide, and gunfire made him dive under the nearest table. It was worse than that, though. At night, he’d sleepwalk, his eyes open, but he wasn’t aware of what he was doing. One night, he stumbled into the saloon half-dressed and waving a gun around. One of the saloon girls knew we were friends and came to fetch me. By the time I got there, he’d been shot in the leg. Even after getting shot, he continued to rage and yell. If I had been minutes later, they would’ve killed him.”

Abigail’s heart ached for the man. “He had a reason to be disturbed. He’d killed people and had to live with that guilt. He saw things no one should have to see.”

“As did you. Those Union soldiers took everything from you as you were forced to watch helplessly. Thunder is a trigger because it mimics cannon fire."

Abigail wanted to hug the man at her side who didn't judge her and instead wanted to help. No one had understood her episodes, not even her sisters. Some of her sisters had night terrors, others didn't want to leave the house, but no one freaked out and went screaming and running down the street during a storm.

"What happened to your friend?" she asked.

Owen smiled. "He married a saloon girl, the one who got me that night. She hid the guns, and locks them inside the house at night. Last I heard, he'd only had one episode in two months. I guess that means he's getting it together."

"Thank you," she said.

"You've faced enough tonight. Let's get you inside." Owen guided her to the door.

Abigail wanted to argue, but thunder clapped with the promise of a heavy storm. "I'll get dinner on the table." She retrieved the biscuits, poured some soup into a bowl, and uncovered the pie she'd collected the berries for earlier.

They sat and ate, Owen devouring the soup and biscuits. "These are great. Thanks."

She nodded and nibbled on her own biscuit, enjoying the saltiness of the meal. “What time do you want to head into town tomorrow?”

“Early, so we can make a long appearance. It’s important that the townspeople see us and know there is nothing going on. I don’t want your reputation to be permanently ruined.”

“I told you—”

“I know you don’t care, but I do. What happens if you want to get a job in town? What if you’re banned from church, or no man will want you because they believe you’re damaged?”

Her temper reared at his words. Didn’t he just kiss her hours ago? It wasn’t a real kiss, but it still meant something. They both felt it, or was she imagining things? She popped the last bite of biscuit in her mouth then shoved her chair back. “I told you I don’t need a man to care for me.” She retrieved both plates, slapped a piece of pie on each and plopped them down on the table again.

“I’m sorry. I didn’t mean to anger you. I know you want your land to be your own, that you don’t need any man to take care of you, but I don’t want to be the cause of you being—”

“Damaged? I heard you.” She ate a few bites of pie, but its sweetness churned her stomach. She abandoned it and crossed her arms over her chest, wishing the storm would stop so she could send him outside to sleep.

Owen rubbed his forehead then placed his fork on the plate. "I only want what's best for you."

"All you want is for me to leave, in whatever manner that happens to be," she said, her voice raised with resentment.

"No. I mean, yes. I believe you'd be safer in town. I thought maybe if I could work your land and mine, get a house built, and give it a year for other homesteaders to arrive, then you could return."

"You can't work both properties by yourself. It takes both of us just to keep the homestead running. And I'm not running away for a year while you work my land. I can handle whatever threatens me or my land."

A clap of thunder made her jump and squeal. Again, Owen was at her side. His arms wrapped around her, holding her tight against him. "Shh. We'll talk about this later."

"There's nothing to talk about. I don't need a man. I don't need you. I don't need anyone." She shoved from his arms and stomped to her side of the dugout. "You can clean the dishes since you think you can run this place without me." She could hear the childishness in her tone, but she didn't care. If he had the nerve to keep trying to belittle her accomplishments on the homestead then he could start doing his own stuff again.

Rain pelted down on the roof of the porch while Owen cleaned the dishes and lowered the lantern light. Droplets fell to the floor, seeping through the earthen roof, so she rose and retrieved a pot to catch the water, while Owen tended to another leak.

"Thank you," he mumbled. "This is going to be a big storm. The wind is uprooting the sod on our roof. Perhaps we can work together on fixing it in the morning."

His sensitive tone soothed her anger. "I can do that, but won't we be late for church?"

He shrugged. "You're right. If the weather's fine after church, we'll be able to work on it then."

She nodded and retreated to her bed. The storm raged on outside and she curled into herself, shaking quietly and hoping he didn't see. The light of the lantern lowered once more until it was only a dull glow in the room. Then a flash of lightning lit the dugout through the cracks in the wood shutters and door. She braced for the loud boom. It came only moments later, pounding through the ground and shaking the dishes and her nerves.

"Here." Owen lifted her with ease from the bed and moved her toward the wall then lay down by her side.

"Aren't you worried about my reputation," she spit his words back at him.

"Right now I'm worried about you." He cradled her head against his chest and held her tight. His lips pressed to the top of her head once again, sending waves of want through her. Another flash of light and she tensed. He squeezed her, bracing for the clap of thunder. For an hour, the storm raged on and Owen protected her from the memories.

"You're doing great," Owen said, no judgment in his tone. "Someday you might even like storms."

Abigail looked up at him as the thunder grew distant. "I used to love storms as a child. My father and I would sit on the front porch and watch the clouds roll in over Kennesaw Mountain. But that was where the cannon fire was the fiercest during the war."

He looked down at her. His fingers caressed her face, leaving a trail of excitement in their wake. "I wish I would've been there to hold you then."

She fought the emotions welling up inside her. "I'm glad you weren't, because then you wouldn't be here today holding me now." Her voice sounded just above a whisper.

Owen nudged her higher on the bed, and she obliged. They lay face to face on the mattress, not saying a word. Only the glow of the dim lantern allowed her to see his strong jaw and promising lips. With the storm fading, she feared he'd move from the bed, and she didn't want that. If she was truthful with herself, she never wanted him to move from her side again.

"Abby, you're so special." He cupped her face and drew her closer.

She hadn't been called Abbey since she left home. His words soothed the loneliness plaguing her soul.

"I'm afraid of you leaving, yet I'm more afraid this prairie will take you from me. I am a man torn between want and need."

She shivered at the seriousness of his gaze and dared to nudge him forward. "What do you need?"

He brushed her hair from her eyes. "I need you to live."

"And what do you want?"

Owen tipped her chin so their lips were closer. “You,” he whispered and pressed his lips to hers with more desire than she’d felt in her lifetime. A heart-thumping, swooning kind of kiss, it was the kind that made you forget about priorities, responsibilities, and promises.

After Owen hitched the horse to the buckboard, he eyed the debris the storm had scattered around the dugout. The wind had been fierce last night, but his desire for Abigail had been fiercer.

The door to the dugout opened and Abigail stepped out in her new church dress. Yards of blue floated from her thin waist. Her red hair dangled in spiraled curls around her pink cheeks. "Beautiful," he murmured under his breath. He offered his hand for her to climb up on the buckboard. "Abigail, you look more beautiful than the north star."

She gathered her skirts and sat on the bench. "No."

He leaned back. "Yes, you're stunning."

"No, I mean call me *Abbey*. I haven't been called that since I left my sisters. I liked it when you whispered that to me last night. When I hear that name, I feel like…I have family around." She toyed with the bonnet resting in her lap.

Owen smiled then rounded the buckboard and hopped up onto the seat beside her. Clicking the reins, he drove toward town, but his mind still slipped back to the memories of last night. The way her body curved into his. "I hope you're not upset that I didn't sleep outside last night."

"Of course not. It was pouring and the straw bed was soaked." Abigail kept her eyes forward on the path ahead.

"I see." Maybe she didn't feel the same about their kiss. It had turned him around and made him want something he never thought possible. Did he dare hope that she felt the same? "Did I…" He straightened the hat on his head. "Did you like…"

"Kissing you?" Abigail lit up at his side. "Yes, but I worried you regretted it. When I woke, you were gone."

He smiled, from the innards of his soul. He couldn't remember the last time he'd felt so relieved and happy. "I'd never regret kissing you. I could kiss you today, tomorrow, any day."

"How about now?" She angled herself to face him with a longing gaze.

"I'm happy to oblige." He released one rein to capture the back of her neck, guiding her lips to his for a kiss that could drive any man insane. A scandalous, sensual kiss that stole his breath and his heart away.

When they finally broke apart, it left them both panting. "Oh my," she stammered, her face flushed and her lips red.

He couldn't speak, or move for a moment as his mind swirled with desire. The horse neighed, drawing his attention to the fact he'd run them off the road and almost into a tree. They both laughed as he backed the horse up and returned to the road to town.

She placed her bonnet on her head as the sun rose higher in the sky. "I think we better keep our kissing to a minimum in public right now."

"I thought you didn't care about what people think?" Owen asked.

She tied the bonnet and dropped her hands to her lap, settling in for the remainder of the ride. "I don't, but that kind of kiss could get us arrested."

He laughed. "I agree."

They rode for a while, and he found himself thinking about the future. In it, he could see the home, the land, and Abigail as his wife. Maybe

Martin was right. Maybe it was time for him to let go of the past and take a chance on the future. "Abbey, do you still feel the same way about men? Are you determined to remain a spinster for life?"

Abigail brushed road dust from her dress and sat silent for a moment. "Part of me still clings to the wish to take care of myself. To prove I don't need a man to make it in this world."

Owen nodded. "What if you didn't need him? What if you *wanted* to work side by side as his partner on a homestead, and in life? You wouldn't be taking care of him, and he wouldn't be taking care of you. You'd be taking care of each other."

She bit her lip, as if battling between what she wanted and what she needed. "I think I'd like a partner in life, but I'm afraid it's not that easy."

Owen's chest cracked under the weight of her words. "Why not?"

She wrung her hands together and opened her mouth, then closed it, but then opened it again. "It's not just me I have to think about."

The buckboard bumped under a large rock, sending Abigail forward on the seat. He scooped her into his side, holding her there so she wouldn't fly out of the wagon. "What are you talking about?" His thoughts flew through possibilities. Was she with child? Had she played him all this time? No, Abigail couldn't do something like that. But then what could it be?

"I have a family in Georgia. My sisters. We have nothing now, because of the war. I don't even know if they are still okay. They could be starving right now. Our situation there is so grave we all chose to be mail-order brides. But I have hope that there's a different way. I begged my sister, Cora, not to allow any of my sisters to leave before I had a chance to make a life for us here. You see, our lands were burned, scorched to the point of being unfertile. And without slaves or my father and brothers we don't have the man power to keep the plantation running anyway. Our home was burnt to the ground as well. So far, we've been surviving on the charity of our neighbors. That's why I need my own land. Without a place to support and care for my sisters, they will be forced to marry. We'll be separated for the rest of our days. And as mail-order brides, they have no idea what kind of husband they could be getting. They could marry men who abuse them, or neglect them." Tears slid down her face. "I can't let that happen. I can't let them down."

Owen mulled over the information. He understood her determination now, but the thought of so many women on his homestead made him want to jump from the moving buckboard and run. Yet, he couldn't, because that would mean he'd have to leave Abigail behind.

"I should've told you before, but I was scared it would make you work harder to get me off my land."

He pulled the horse to a stop at the edge of town. "I won't do that. I promise I won't take your land from you. We'll figure out how to build a house big enough for all of us." He couldn't believe his own words, but all he knew is that he wanted a new life, one with a family. And by bringing her sisters here he'd have an instant family.

Hearing another buckboard come from behind, he said, "We'll speak more on our way home. For now, you should know that I think you have stolen my heart, and I want to know you better. If that means bringing your sisters here, then we'll find a way. Abbey, trust me. I won't fail you."

Chapter Sixteen

Buckboards, wagons, and horses congregated outside a white-washed building with a cross on top. Smaller than the churches back in Georgia, Abigail wondered if it could fit even half of the people in town. Men and women in their Sunday finest made their way into the building while others climbed down from their buggies and joined their neighbors.

Abigail's nerves were rougher than the road on the way into town. It was easy to not care what people thought of her when she didn't have to face them. A blonde young woman, holding a baby, eyed her, then whispered into her husband's ear.

Owen pulled their buckboard to a halt and helped her down. Conversations of Indians, mill work, taxes, and homesteads swirled through the crowd as she made her way up the stairs and into the church. She spotted Susan, and they joined her and Martin at the pew. Martin offered his hand to Owen. “Thought you might need a friend to back you.”

“I won’t turn it down.”

The preacher plopped his Bible down on the pulpit with a loud thump. Owen settled in by Abigail’s side.

“Welcome, everyone. It’s so good to see you all come out this fine Sunday morning. Before we get started, there are a few town announcements. Mrs. Wallaby?”

The woman who’d been whispering into her husband’s ear passed the baby to a friend and took her place at the front. “We’re collecting donations to help the mill workers’ wives manage during this difficult time. Please, if you’d like to contribute, see me after service. We’re going to provide comfort, food, and any other help to those in need.” She nodded to the preacher and stepped down, but paused before taking her seat.

“If we keep letting them Injuns set fire to our town, there won’t be anything left soon,” her husband added.

The preacher returned to his pulpit, but tugged at his collar as if the man’s words choked him.

"Yes, well, we will always have room in our hearts for any fellow Christian who has fallen and wishes to ask for God's forgiveness. If that is all for today—"

Owen stood and Abigail wanted to yank him back to her side. She wanted to protect him from the men and women glaring at his interruption. "No, I have something to add. It's about the attack on the mill."

The men nodded their agreement, and Abigail had no doubt they hoped he would join the cause to hunt and kill all the Indians in the area.

"This land is still wild and untamed," Owen continued, "but we all work hard to break ground on a new life." Heads nodded their agreement. Abigail's pulse roared, wild and untamed. She fought to hear over the thumping in her ears. "What we forget is that the Indians once lived on this very land. Their dead are buried in nearby fields. Their homes are now gone. Their brothers, sisters, husbands, and wives were sacrificed for our progress."

"You a savage lover?" Someone in the back of the congregation hollered.

"No, I'm a lover of all of God's children, and I believe He weeps for every man injured or lost to us at the mill attack."

A man with a shaggy beard slapped his knee with his hat. "Not following you, boy. You want to kill them savages or not?"

Martin turned in his seat to face the man. "Let the man speak and he'll explain." The congregation appeared to respect Martin enough to settle and listen.

"I want to save lives," Owen said. "Each time we attack them, they retaliate. And each time they attack us, we retaliate. I don't know about all of you, but I'm tired of war and death."

"Me, too," a small voice from nearby said. A frail whisper of a woman stood. "I lost my first husband and my eldest son to the war, then another son to an accident on the wagon train coming through here. I'm not about to lose what I've managed to build in Prairie City. My husband who works to clear our land for planting, my younger son who works alongside him, or the baby I carry. Please, sir. Tell us how we can end this senseless fighting and death."

"By not provoking the Indians anymore, by leaving them alone. If we allow them to remain on the other side of the creek and leave them in peace, then we'll be left in peace. No more attacks on the mill or any homestead around Prairie City."

Abigail watched Owen plead with the men in the church. She willed them to listen to reason, but why would they? Men seldom chose peace over war, as if their pride would not allow them to see sense and reason. She imagined the Indian woman having the same issue with her own people. Did Indians value a woman's opinion anymore than white men did? Did they have rights?

"How'd this treaty occur?" the preacher asked.

Owen turned his attention to the man they both knew could persuade the good people of Prairie City either for or against their cause. "A woman and her child spoke to us near our homestead."

"You speak savage?" the man with the shaggy beard said, spitting his outrage more than speaking.

Abigail couldn't stay silent. She'd never been good at remaining quiet when there was a purpose. "No, but her son speaks some words in our language. Through him, we were able to reach this agreement."

"What does a Southern rich girl like you understand about Indians and worrying about them killing you in your sleep," a woman in a pink bonnet said.

The room quieted, and all gazes rested on her. "You're right. I came from a plantation in Georgia where we had the finest dresses and as much food as we could eat. Until war came. My land was scorched, our house burned, my brothers murdered. I should be the first to trust no one, yet I'm willing to bet my land on this agreement," Abigail said, her temper rising.

The congregation erupted in conversation, but the preacher banged his hand against the pulpit until silence returned.

"This woman comes into our town and spouts these ridiculous notions. She's obviously already worked her wiles on Mr. Baker," the woman with the baby said.

Owen whirled around and the woman's husband bolted upright to defend her. Abigail clutched Owen's shirt. His muscles strained against the material and her plea to sit down.

"Mrs. Wallaby, please take your seat. Everyone, please take your seat. There will be no lynching in my church today. As for the town news of the Indians, we all have suffered great loss. I believe our town council should consider Mr.

Baker's proposal after checking in with the families who have lost loved ones at the mill. For today, on God's holy day, there will be no conflict. This is a house of God and it is time for us to pray for all those who have suffered the loss of loved ones. Please bow your heads."

The preacher's words seemed to soothe the parishioners, if only for the duration of the service. Abigail prayed for the Indians, for her sisters, for Owen and the trouble she'd brought to him. She'd been so devoted and focused on her plans for her family that she never considered the ruin it could bring upon Owen. She wanted to cry for letting him close to her. If she didn't think so fondly of him, this wouldn't be so difficult to endure.

The service continued in silence, but Abigail could feel the congregation's hatred boring into the back of her head. All she wanted to do was return to her homestead and never step foot in Prairie City again. But that wouldn't be possible. She would need supplies eventually, not to mention the post office. No, she wouldn't let these townspeople run her out of town, or ruin anything else.

When the service ended, Martin and Susan remained by their sides as the congregation filed out the front doors. The clacking of shoes on the steps told her when the last of them exited. The preacher joined them with a warm smile. “Hi. I wanted to introduce myself. I’m Brother Elijah. Welcome to Prairie City.”

Owen shook his hand then the preacher smiled and nodded at Abigail.

“I must caution you two. There are many people in this town who have taken it upon themselves to enforce the laws, if not create some of their own.” He tucked his Bible to his chest and nodded at each of them.

Abigail sighed. “Thank you for your concern.”

Preacher Elijah shook Martin’s hand and smiled at Susan. “I’m glad you both could make it today. It’s always a pleasure to see you here.”

Martin tucked Susan into his side. “We try to come as often as we can. Afraid work has got us tied up, what with preparing our land and building.”

Susan scooted toward Preacher Elijah. “We’d love to have you for dinner again soon, though.”

Elijah scanned the room then moved closer. “I’d love that, but don’t tell anyone. I’m afraid doctor advised me to cut down on the dinner invitations after the last two. I fear my stomach and Mrs. Maulden’s soup do not get along.” He turned to Owen and Abigail and nodded. “Good day. I hope to see you here again next Sunday." The young man seemed wiser than his years. Perhaps God truly guided him in his chosen path. "If you ever need my services, I would be happy to oblige." The man winked, a strange gesture for a preacher. She couldn't imagine Preacher John from Georgia winking. There would've been a scandal.

"I need to take care of a few things." Owen put his hand on the small of her back, sending warmth up her spine. "We thought maybe Susan and you could post your letters while I take care of something at the at the store."

Susan nodded and offered her arm to Abigail. "Sounds like the men have important business to tend to." Her mocking tone made her husband shake his head.

Both women made their way through the crowds on the street to the post office. She quickly noticed that there appeared to be five men to every one female in town. Perhaps some of these men were looking for brides. If she brought her sisters out here, maybe they could marry men they chose for themselves, instead of ending up with complete strangers. That way they would stay close as well and not scatter all over the territories.

"I see now why there are mail-order bride services."

Susan nudged into her side. "That's how most of these women ended up here."

"Really?" Abigail asked.

Susan nodded. They reached the post office and to Abigail's relief it was open. A woman sorting mail behind a desk greeted them as they entered. "Good morning."

Abigail retrieved her letters from her bag. "I'd like to post these to Marietta, Georgia please."

"Certainly, ma'am." She glanced at the envelopes and smiled. "So you are Abigail McKinnie. I actually have mail for you."

Abigail's heart soared to the sky. She could barely keep from leaping over the desk to get a letter from home.

"Here you go."

Abigail thanked her then ripped open the letter and faded into her own world, the script of her dearest sister, Cora, uplifting her spirits.

My Dearest Sister,

I hope all is well in Prairie City and our cousin, Mr. O'Brien, is treating you well. Perhaps you've even persuaded him to allow you to work the land without marriage. I must admit I have my doubts, though. Even still, I know your powers of persuasion. I've seen you convince many into doing things to help our family when they had little for themselves.

I fear the news I have will greatly upset you, but I must tell you. Josephine is not well. Her emotions are unstable here. She cannot remain in Georgia a day longer than necessary. I've chosen a God-fearing family in Colorado with great means. I know that is not your wish, but I felt it was the best option. I've also sold the land that remains to the Whitakers at a robbery price, but it'll be enough to provide a decent dowry. Josephine assures me this is what she wishes for her future, a place far from the horrors of war and the memories of that Union soldier who ruined her. We both know that finding a good man who will want her as a wife is nearly impossible here. I chose Colorado since there will be no one that knows of her past. We've spoken, and she's agreed it best to keep her secret and marry the son of a hotel owner, a wealthy man who is invested in railroads and hotels. She will find happiness if only in the form of material comforts. I only hope she can tolerate a man's touch again.

By the time you read this letter, I will be making arrangements for her departure and I fear you will not be able to offer us any hope in time. Please know you have sacrificed greatly for us, and we will always love you, but it is time that we find our own way. I will write with more news soon.

Love,

Cora

Abigail collapsed onto the steps outside the post office, her legs too weak with anguish to move. She'd failed to protect her baby sister from the Union soldier, and now she'd failed to protect her from having to marry a man she didn't know. A man who could be as brutal as the one that took her virtue.

Owen shook Mr. Graham's hand and joined him at the counter. "I've spoken to Johnson at the claims office and he assures me that a woman can own land under the new Homestead Act."

Relief flooded Owen. That meant they could build a house on her land and work side by side to make both one-hundred-and-sixty acre tracks flourish.

"As long as she was married, of course," Mr. Graham added.

More customers entered the store, but Owen couldn't move. How could he tell Abigail she couldn't keep her land, not under the current law since she'd never married Willy O'Brien.

"I'm sorry if this news distresses you," Mr. Graham said.

Martin patted his shoulder. “You gonna tell Ms. McKinnie the news?”

“I know I need to, but the thought of crushing her dreams puts a knot in my gut. She’s worked so hard. She’ll succeed in getting her homestead to thrive within five years per the Homesteading Act requirements, I have no doubt. I can’t claim that about most men.” He slammed his fist down on the counter, causing the other patrons to stare.

“Let’s take a walk.” Martin plopped his hat on his head and gestured toward the door.

Owen nodded, the store suddenly feeling too crowded.

“Before you leave, I have some more notes from him.” Mr. Graham handed him a small piece of paper with more laws scribbled on it.

Owen stuffed it into his pocket then shuffled out into the sunshine. “How am I going to tell Abbey?”

“Abbey?” Martin raised an eyebrow at him. “I think there’s an obvious solution here.”

A spark of hope drew Owen’s attention. “What’s that?”

Shaking his head, Martin smacked his shoulder. “Marry her. Then she can share your land.”

Owen drooped with disappointment. "Even if I wanted to marry her, which I don't know if I do, she would never agree. The point is that she owns her own land, that she controls her own destiny. She's suffered so much, she deserves her own land."

"You both have." Martin adjusted his hat on his head to shield his eyes from the bright sunlight. "Looks like you can talk about it. There's the women now."

Owen glanced up and instantly saw the pain in Abigail's eyes. His heart lurched. Did she already know? A wagon drove by between them, but he saw her clutch something to her chest. He made his way through the horses and people to the other side of the road and squatted by her side. "What is it? What's wrong?"

Abigail opened her mouth then glanced at Susan. Lowering the paper, she closed her mouth, folded it and stood. "We should be heading back to the homestead before it gets too late."

Susan placed her arm around Abigail's shoulders and walked with her to the buckboard, leaving Owen feeling lost and confused. "She knows," he mumbled.

Martin adjusted his belt. "Doubt that."

They followed the women to the front of the church where only a few men lingered. He helped Abigail onto the buckboard then turned to Susan.

She only offered a weary smile. “It’s not my place to say, but give her time. Sometimes things are too awful to say aloud.”

His gut twisted and knotted with the thought of Abigail suffering anything too terrible to say aloud. He glanced around and knew this wasn’t the place to discuss such things, so he shook Martin’s hand and joined Abigail for a silent ride out of town. She clutched the letter tight as if it were the last chance at happiness. By the time they passed the downed tree a mile outside Prairie City, he couldn’t take it any longer. “Please, Abigail. Tell me how I can help you. The sorrow you carry is too much for me to watch. I’ll do anything to help you. Trust me.”

Her straight posture and blank stare didn’t waiver, so he continued until the fork in the path leading to their homestead. Maybe Martin was right and he should consider marriage again. He sighed and shifted in his seat, the weight of his words too heavy to carry. It would just be him saving another girl in distress. That never worked. Yet, the thought of Abigail by his side for the rest of his days made him feel as if he could touch the clouds in the sky.

"My sister," she mumbled with tears streaming down her face. He'd never seen her cry, not when the Indians attacked her, not when she'd walked all those miles to the homestead, not from blisters or lack of sleep. His insides melted into a sludgy mess.

"What about your sister?" He pulled the buckboard to a stop, needing to touch her, to make her pain disappear. With both her hands in his, he willed her to share what ailed her. "I meant it. You can trust me. I want to share this burden with you."

"I fear no one can share her burden. I'm realizing that now. I tried. I held her at night when the nightmares ravaged her the way…" She broke into light sobs and he pulled her into him, holding her as she cried. His skin prickled with the thought of what happened. From her dark tone, he knew it was grave.

"Let me get you home. I'll make us some coffee, and we can sit and talk. You know of my past, what scars I suffer. I want to help mend yours."

She pulled from him and straightened to her rigid posture again. "I'm fine." She retrieved a handkerchief from her bag and dabbed at her eyes. "I will just have to work harder."

"No woman or man could work any harder than you do." He took her hand once more. It trembled under his touch. "I know I set you up to fail, but you've proven yourself more capable than anyone I know. It's okay to lean on someone, Abbey. It won't make you weak. In fact, it'll make you stronger."

He drove on to the dugout and helped Abigail down. She headed for the creek, so he abandoned the task of unloading the wagon and followed her to a rock where she sat. They remained quiet for several minutes with only the sound of the trickling water to fill the silence. At a loss for what to do, he placed a hand on her back and rubbed small circles until she relaxed into his touch. "You can trust me with anything, Abbey. I would never betray you."

She shivered and clutched the letter tighter. "My sister…she's leaving for out west to marry."

His chest tightened at the way she said *marry*, as if it were the worst fate on earth. She truly hated the thought, didn't she? "Perhaps your sister doesn't feel the same about marriage that you do. Some women wish to marry."

"It's not that." She swallowed as if to stall her next words. "What if he turns her away? I don't know if she could handle that."

Owen tried to calm the million questions raging through his mind and allow her a moment to share. He leaned his head against hers and rubbed the back of her neck. Her hair smelled of fresh flowers in summer, her skin softer than a sunflower petal. "I'm here for you."

"He's from a good and well-to-do family."

He struggled to follow her words, to understand what the issue was. "You don't want her taken care of?"

"Of course, I do. I'm happy if she finds an easier life than what we've had the last few years. It's not that." Abigail rotated her head and he could see her dark lashes flutter closed. "It would be the best of circumstances if it were real, but I fear the truth will cause him to send her away. I fear she could not handle being shamed again. I should've done more. I should've protected her. It's my fault. I let those soldiers into our home, but I saw no other choice. If I had turned them away, they probably would've killed us." Her shoulders shook with sobs. "It's my fault she's ruined."

His pulse fired with anger. "A soldier forced her?" He heard the disgust in his own voice. If there was one thing he could never tolerate it was a man taking advantage of a woman.

She moved her head down then up only slightly, but it was enough to confirm. “Were you?”

“No.” She backed away. “But I would’ve traded places with her if I could. I would rather I live with the shame, with never receiving a man’s love or getting married. I would suffer ten attacks to take the one from my baby sister.” Her breath came in gulps of air.

Owen touched her knee, just to have contact with her, as if the break in their connection would shatter his heart. “Not all men would care of such things. Perhaps the man she’s promised to will understand it wasn’t her fault and that she is special for being able to live through such a horrible incident.”

Abigail stilled, her sobs faded to small gasps of air until she regained control and turned to him, her eyes full of question. “Would you?”

“Would I what?”

Abigail lifted her chin like she always did when she prepared for the worst. “Accept a woman who wasn’t pure?”

Owen took both her arms, gripped them tight and turned her toward him. “You listen to me now, Abigail McKinnie. If you had suffered this fate, it would make no difference to me. It would never be a reason not to marry you. In fact, I'd only love you more for facing life head on after such horrific circumstances. That thought would never tarnish the beauty of who you are. Your hair would still be the color of the sun that makes me smile in the morning. Your eyes would still be the color of the most beautiful gem ever mined. Your body would still call to me, your lips as soft and delicious. Nothing could ever take that away from you. Ever."

Her chest rose and fell in labored breaths. "You mean that, don't you?"

"Every word." Owen leaned closer, longing for her lips on his. "Neither of us were looking for another, but I believe the good Lord above guided you here. You stumbled onto my land as well as into my heart for a reason. I understand now why you don't want a man. Because of your guilt for your sister, you will not love a man because you fear your sister will never have that. It's time for you to stop punishing yourself, Abbey. It's time for us both to stop punishing ourselves."

She bit her bottom lip and searched the ground, the sky, his eyes as if looking for answers then she smiled and whispered two words that drove him nearly mad with happiness. "Kiss me."

For a week, Abigail worked side-by-side with Owen to build their new home on the property. This one they chose to build without a sod roof that leaked, or fell on your face at night. Nor of bricks from the ground that attracted mice and rattlesnakes. It was extravagant to purchase wood and extra work to transport logs from the wooded area across the creek, but it was starting to feel like a real home.

She heaved the axe once more to make a notch in the log and Owen worked at the other end making a notch of his own. "Do you think this will be big enough for all seven of you?"

She hit the wood once more and a brown chunk flew into the air. "It'll be more than we had."

Owen chopped three more times for each of her one swings. "We could extend out the side to make another room."

She shook her head. "We went from a mansion to a two room, burnt-out house, with the windows broken and half of one wall blasted out. This will be luxury to them. And don't worry. They'll work the land, too. Trust me. With all of us working together, we'll be able to make the five-year agreement on both our lands."

The wind picked up and she feared another storm was coming, but in the last few days the rumbling thunder hadn't made her crazy, only on edge. A hint of a cool breeze skirted over the prairie grass, making it dance. She loved the open lands and the privacy.

"I think you're right. Only I don't think the home will be big enough for all seven of you."

"I told you not to worry. We'll be fine." She finished her notch a few dozen strokes behind Owen, but he never crowded her or hurried her to finish. She loved that about him. His patience was like no other man she'd ever known.

Owen took her axe from her hand and tossed it to the ground next to his own. "I don't want you to have that in your hand when I ask you this." He cupped her cheek the way she loved, with his palm cradling her face. "I want to assure you this is not because I don't think you can handle your own land, or because you're not strong enough to run your own house. It's because you're so strong at everything you do."

Abigail eyed the approaching storm and the work they still had to complete. "What are you getting at, Owen? I'm not sure I like how it's starting."

"I know, but I hope you like how it ends." Owen took a long breath and his hands shook against her face.

Her breath hitched at the apprehensive tightening of his jaw. "What is it? What's wrong?"

"Nothing. Everything." Owen chuckled. "I'm not doing a good job with this." He cleared his throat and guided her to sit on the log while he paced in front of her for a second and then dropped to his knees in front of her, taking her hands in his. "Abbey, I have never loved a woman. Yes, I've been married, but it was to save her from a fate I believed unbearable. When you stumbled onto my land—"

"My land," she teased to keep herself from assuming too much. Her heart had already sped up with anticipation for something her brain told her to run from.

"Our land. At least, I hope it'll all be our land. I want your sisters to move here to be by your side, so that you'll be able to let go of your guilt and be happy. So, you'll be able to allow yourself to love a man and trust him. A man like me, Abbey." He clung to her hands and gazed into her eyes. "I hope you'll consider a future with me. Trust me to never take anything from you. To only love and support you."

"I do," Abbey breathed.

"As my wife," Owen said, his voice strong and promising almost commanding. Yet, she didn't mind.

Her emotions churned from guilt to hope to love. "Yes, I'll marry you, Owen Baker. I'd be proud to be your wife."

He lifted her into his arms and swung her around, ending with a toe-curling, impatient kind of kiss. When they broke for air, he held her face and smiled. "We'll go tomorrow to send word for your sisters to move here, and have the preacher marry us. I can't wait another minute, and I certainly can't continue to sleep under the same roof with you without wanting more. A man can only take so much torture." His hungry gaze traveled the length of her body, heating her with passion.

"I agree." She kissed him once more and the thunder rolled over the prairie. She didn't care. Nothing would ruin this moment.

They managed to finish their work in between stolen kisses and touches then entered the dugout as the rain pelted onto their leaky roof. "We should live here and let my sisters have the house."

"I can't have you live in this hovel forever. It's only temporary. We'll add an extension onto the house or build a small cabin for us."

Abigail took him into her arms. "I could live anywhere if it's with you."

Bam, Bam, Bam.

Abigail jumped at the knock on the door. Owen grabbed his rifle and peered out the window. "It's Indians."

She tensed and they both stood, eyeing the door.

Bam, bam, bam.

Owen handed her the rifle. "I don't think they'd knock if they meant us harm. I'm going to see what they want, but anything goes wrong, shoot."

She took the rifle and settled it at her shoulder, ready to fire. Owen wrenched the door open and stepped back. The young boy they had met a few weeks earlier by the creek stood on the front porch with a man. “Help.”

The older man stumbled into the door and collapsed. Owen pulled him inside, eyed the surrounding terrain and then shut the door. He placed the wood beam back in its slat to keep out any other danger. “Help me get him onto the table.”

Blood dyed the dirt floor dark and the smell of open wounds stirred her fear. She took one arm and helped Owen heave the man onto the table. Her arms strained under the weight of him, but she’d grown stronger working her land. “What happened?”

“White men attack,” the young boy said, tears streaking down his dirty face. “Said we burned farm. No burn.”

Owen analyzed the wound and gathered supplies from the kitchen. “He can’t stay here. We need to fix him up and get him back to his people. If we’re caught with him here, there’s no telling what’ll happen.”

Abigail took the cloth Owen handed her and pressed it to the wound in his side until the bleeding slowed. “You didn’t burn the farm?”

“No. Agreed no attack.”

The agreement had worked. The Indian woman had managed to convince her people, only to have Abigail and Owen fail to stop their own neighbors.

"What farm?"

The boy pointed toward the back of the dugout. "Two homes."

"That's the Wallaby place."

She quirked a brow at him. "Who?"

"The man, woman, and baby who sat behind us at church last Sunday."

They worked on mending the bleeding Indian on their table while the boy stood in the corner shivering from fear. Why did men have to keep killing each other?

"I believe the boy," she said in a low voice.

Owen nodded as he wrapped cloth around the man's stomach. "Me, too. I'll go out tomorrow and see what I find."

Abigail eyed the scared child and wished she could do more. "How will we get them back to their people?"

"Men wait. Guard trees and creek." The boy crossed his arms over his chest. The tears had dried up, a hint of a grown man's anger showing in his set jaw.

"We can't just send him out to walk back. He'll be shot on sight. I'm sure the men have already decided to lynch them or shoot them." Owen cleaned up the supplies and leaned against the back wall, thinking for a moment. "My clothes. We'll dress him in my clothes and when the rain stops and he awakens, we'll help him to the creek. He'll need to cross and make it into the woods before the men realize he's not one of the posse. With a hat and my clothes and the darkness, I think it'll work."

"What about the boy?" Abigail asked.

"We'll have to put him in something, too. Grab my clothes and I'll go get a horse blanket from the barn to cover his shoulders with. It should do in the darkness long enough to get him across the creek and into the woods." Owen unbolted the door and disappeared into the stormy night. She didn't like him being out there alone, but they both had a job to do. She went to the back of the dugout and retrieved his other pair of pants, his Sunday best. She'd get fabric to make him a new pair when they went into town tomorrow.

The boy sat by the man's side as he slept and she could see the father-son bond between them. She only wished the boy had been able to face less in his young life. If only they could all live in peace.

She grabbed Owen's pants and a piece of paper fell from the pocket. She picked it up and opened it to see if it was important.

Homestead Act Laws

An unmarried woman has no rights to own land.

Abigail read the words, but couldn't make her brain register them. She read on in hopes of finding a reason.

To answer Mr. Baker's question, yes, the land will be returned to public ownership if said owner was unmarried without children. If the land was deeded to Mr. Baker from Mr. O'Brien, then he may have a claim if no others dispute it.

Owen had been lying to her. Why else would he consult a lawyer about land rights regarding her land?

Her temper ignited and she waited for Owen to return before she erupted. No man would use her and toss her away. She'd fight, fight to the death to save her land and not even Owen Baker would stop her. Not with his smooth talking and false promises of love.

Chapter Nineteen

On his way back from the barn, Owen spotted men racing through the prairie toward his home and his breath caught. If they found the Indian in their dugout they'd be facing retaliation at the very least, or they'd swing from the nearest tree at the worst.

A strange howl sounded in the distance, more man than dog. One of the horses reared and the men made a sharp left and headed toward the creek. He released his breath and collapsed against the side of the dugout. The thought of mixing Abigail up in this, the danger he'd put her in, made him dizzy with regret. He watched until the clouds shrouded the moonlight making the land turn black. This would be their best chance to execute his plan.

He saddled a horse so it looked like a white man rode it and returned with the horse blanket for the boy. To his relief, the man had woken up and was drinking water with the boy at his side. The love between father and son was undeniable. He never thought he'd have that, but now he dared to dream.

Abigail held up Owen's coat and the man slipped his arm in with a cringe and grunt, but they managed to get him dressed before he collapsed back into a chair. Owen doubted he'd make the ride to the woods, but what choice did they have?

The boy held his hand tight and pulled him to his feet, saying something in their native tongue. Abigail placed a hat on his head, and Owen noticed her hand tremble. She was stressed, her face tight with worry.

"It'll be okay. Trust me," he reassured her.

She took the horse blanket from his hands and wrapped it around the boy. "You better get moving."

He took both her hands. "Don't worry."

She yanked her hands from his grasp. "I can take care of myself."

"Please, don't shut me out now. I know you can. We'll make it through this together. I promise." He edged closer to her, but she backed away again.

"You also promised you didn't want my land. You told me I could trust you," she said, backing away from him as if he suffered prairie madness.

The Indian gave him a look like he should run for it before his woman clobbered him. "I don't understand. I didn't know the Indians would come here. I didn't mean to stir up trouble for us."

She shook her head, her red ringlets swinging around her face like flames. "You tried to steal my land."

"No. I wouldn't." Owen ran a hand through his hair, trying to figure out why she made such an accusation. "I would never take from you."

She shot her hand out in front of her, holding a small piece of paper. "What's this then? You're going to pretend you know nothing about it? That you didn't lie to me? That you didn't pretend to love me in order to steal my land?"

"What are you talking about?" He reached for the paper and she tossed it at him. It glided to the dirt floor, so he bent down to retrieve it. Once he saw the writing, he remembered.

"It was in your pants pocket. Don't deny it isn't yours."

"It's mine," Owen mumbled, catching up to the events that led to this moment. The moment where he saw the woman he loved look at him with more disgust than Mr. Wallaby did when Indians were mentioned.

"So, you don't deny it. I guess the lies have finally caught up with you."

Owen dropped the paper onto the table and stepped toward her, but she shuffled away from him. "Abbey—"

"Don't call me that. Only the people I love can call me that."

Her words thundered through his ears, pierced his heart and ricocheted into his gut where it thudded harder than a horse kick. Pain saturated his innards. "Please. Let me explain."

"Explain what? That you're building a house for my sisters even though they'd never live there? You wanted to keep me from marrying another man so I couldn't claim my land?"

"No. I wanted to protect you. I'd hoped I was wrong." Owen paced the floor, eyeing the danger at his right and more at his left. Which did he face first?

Men's shouts forced him to choose. "We'll have to discuss this later. The horse is around the side of the house. I'll get him saddled and walk them as far as the creek. You stay here. Don't leave." He moved close to her, grabbing her arms despite her protest. He'd never manhandled a girl before, but he couldn't let her go, not until he fully explained. "Promise me you'll stay and wait."

She opened her mouth to protest, but the sound of galloping horses cut her off. He bolted for the window, his heart thrashing against his chest. "They're headed straight here."

He beat his hand against the wall and bits of sod fell on his head. With one room and one window and door at the front, there would be no escape. "Abigail, hide under the bed." He grabbed his rifle and turned to fight, but the door was already open and Abigail was gone.

Chapter Twenty

The darkness covered the posse. Abigail could only see the outline of coats and hats. She raced from the door, running as far as she could get away from the dugout. "Help! Please, help me."

She stumbled over her skirts, landing face down in sludge. One of the men jumped down from the horse and helped her up. "What is it, ma'am?"

Her mind flickered through options to keep them from discovering the father and son inside. She didn't want to add more ammo to an already intense hatred for the Indian's, but she knew one way to get them away from the dugout. "Indian… He came after me. Owen tried to fight him off. He told me to run. They're in the shed around back of the house. I'm afraid he's gonna scalp him." She clawed at the man, thankful it was too dark to see her face. "Please, you have to help him before it's too late."

"Stay here. We'll get that savage." The deep voice of the man from church echoed in the night. She held her breath and waited, hoping that the men would pass the dugout and go straight for the shed. She wasn't even sure why she cared, but a part of her hoped there was an explanation to the note she'd found in Owen's pocket. If not, it had all been a lie. Even still, she couldn't watch another man die.

She followed the men toward the shed and lit the lantern hanging on the nail outside. "Please, don't let anything happen to Owen."

"Guess the boy learned his lesson," Mr. Wallaby said. The other men laughed their agreement.

"Listen, ma'am. You wait out here. We don't want nothing happenin' to you." A man she hadn't met before nudged her to the other side of the horses and in the flash of light that lit the sky, she saw the men head into the shed. She backed away. With another flash of light, she saw the front door of the dugout open then shut, and she knew it was Owen with the Indian and the boy.

"No one's here, ma'am."

She dug deep for her old Southern belle ways, exaggerating her distress for attention and turned around in all directions with the back of her hand to her head. “Oh no, where can he be? That savage must’ve taken him.” Another flash of light and she stopped eyeing the distant field. “Wait.” She stumbled forward, pretending to almost collapse in front of them.

“What?”

“I saw something, in the prairie grass out there. A man, I think, with feathers on his head. It’s gotta be him.” She ran forward and screamed, “Owen!”

One of the men grabbed hold of her and held her back. “I need you to stay here, ma’am. We’ll catch him. You two, head for the field. He can’t get far. I’ll keep my eyes peeled and at the next flash of light, we’ll see him good enough.”

“If not, we best head for shelter. That wind’s picking up something fierce. I don’t want to be stuck out here with a twister coming.”

“Stop being such a coward, Lenard,” Mr. Wallaby ordered. He moved out of the lantern light with his side shooter drawn, aiming at the darkness.

For a long minute, there was no light, no sound, no indication of Owen’s escape. The electricity in the air prickled the hair on her skin and a flash of light struck the ground in the distance. The subsequent rumble funneled underground through the prairie grass as if a great monster threatened to suck them down to Hell. She squirmed at the noise, but Lenard kept hold.

A grunt sounded beyond the dugout and she felt the man loosen his grip and move toward the noise, so she swooned. Landing in his arms, she lay limp and he lowered her to the ground. “Ma’am, wake up.” He tapped her face, but at the next sound, he abandoned her on the ground and drew his gun. Before she could even breathe, he took off to the dugout and out of her sight. She held her breath then heard the smack of a hand on a horse, a neigh and then the thuds of hooves galloping away. She prayed he’d escaped. All of them.

The lightning flashed again and she saw the Indian and the boy ride the horse across the front pasture and disappear into the darkness. “Over here,” the man called from the dugout.

They’d know now. She only hoped Owen had escaped, too. She backed into the shadows and ran for the ditch near the outhouse to hide, the closest hiding place she could manage while remaining out of sight.

"I found the Injun lover. He's gonna pay for this. He'll be hanged in the morning. Sent the Indian on his own horse to escape." Mr. Wallaby shoved Owen toward another who punched him in the gut. Lantern light shone on three of the men, the others on the edge of it, harder to see.

Mr. Wallaby waved toward the dugout. "Check inside." One of the men beyond the lantern light ran in that direction, his footsteps echoing. "What about the woman?"

Lenard eyed the ground where she'd been lying moments earlier and he took off his hat and hit his knee with it. "Dang it to all, she was in on it, too."

"Sir." The man returned from the house and stepped into the circle of light with bloodied rags in his hands. "Doesn't look like that savage is gonna get far."

The wind picked up. The sound of something barreling through the fields drowned out their voices. Another flash of light and she saw the men all together, Owen in between them, and they didn't look happy. She strained to hear, but the wind was too loud.

Beyond the lantern light, the men mounted their horses. "Let's get to my farm," hollered Mr. Wallaby.

She strained to hear more, but the noise of the wind grew louder. It sounded like a train. Only muffled shouts reached her ears and then another flash of light shot across the sky. Lenard looked straight at her and she knew she'd been caught. She ducked and turned, looking for somewhere to run at the next flash of light. But there was nowhere to run. A huge, dark funnel of swirling anger tore through the pasture in a direct path with the outhouse, with her, with everyone. It screamed into the night and with every flash of light she saw it closed in on her. Debris flew in sharp chunks, bits of fencing and homes. She crouched down and cried out for help, but no one could hear her muffled pleas.

They rode hard and fast to the Wallaby farm, leaving the twister and Abigail behind. Owen thought he'd caught a glimpse of her near the outhouse, but he wasn't sure. The thought of her out in that storm, knowing her fears, tore him up. He needed to get back to her, but how? Even if he could untie his hands and leap from the horse, he'd never be able to get away without getting shot. Not to mention he'd only lead the posse right back to Abigail. He struggled anyway, fighting to free his hands. The rope seared his skin, but he kept going until they reached Wallaby's homestead. Blood trickled down his arm from the cuts from the rope fibers.

"Not goin' anywhere so you might as well give up. We'll keep you here until morning then turn you over to the law," Lenard said.

"We're not turning him over to the law." Wallaby sneered at Owen. "Not when he turned a savage loose. A savage that attacked my home, scared my child and threatened my wife. If I would've been seconds later, he would've done horrible things to my family. No, we're gonna determine his fate in the morning. A rope and a tree would be far less troublesome than court and jail."

"We can't—"

"We can," Wallaby snapped. "There's no law out here. The city's miles away and we need to protect our land. No one's going to even care that this man was punished. Now tie him up in the shed and guard him until morning. Once this storm lets up and we can see, we'll head back out to find that savage." Wallaby walked away then paused a few steps from him. "And the girl. She needs to be punished, too."

Owen lurched forward, but the other men held him back. "You can't touch her. She knew nothing. You'll be harming an innocent woman."

"Oh, we both know that woman ain't innocent. Doesn't matter, though. She broke the law, the law of our land, and she needs to pay the price." Wallaby disappeared toward his soddie where a baby cried.

Why would the Indians target his home made of sod, and the barn? Owen scanned the field, but couldn't see much. If his suspicions were correct, the animals were still safe in the barn and no real damage was done. That didn't sound like Indians.

Owen strained and kicked, bucking to try and free himself. He had to get to Abigail. He had no doubt that his words at church had prompted this drama. He couldn't let another woman die because of him. Especially a woman he loved, a woman who thought he'd betrayed her.

The men dragged him to the shed and tied his feet, too.

"Settle down. You're only going to hurt yourself more," Lenard said.

"Hurt myself? I'm not going to accept being hanged at sun up. If I get free, you all better run." Owen struggled, unable to accept his fate. Nothing and no one was going to keep him from Abigail. He wasn't going to let anything happen to her.

"He's just trying to scare you." Lenard eyed the door with a concerned furrow of his brow.

Owen shook his head and leaned against the sod wall. "Then you're naive. That man has a deep hatred for anyone not like him. Those Indians didn't attack his land. He's lying."

"Of course, they did. His outhouse was burned and the tree next to his house." Lenard puffed out his chest as if that was the final word on the matter.

"Really? And why do you think the Indians would bother to burn down an outhouse when they've burned down mills, sheds, and homes before? It's convenient that there are no witnesses, and his property is barely affected by this so-called attack."

The man scratched his head. "No, that's crazy talk."

"Crazy is lynching an innocent man. And you being a member of this posse makes you guilty of murder. You know what they do to murders, don't you?"

The man shuffled to the door. "You're just trying to convince me to let you go, but I ain't gonna do that. You let that savage escape, and now he'll come back and kill my family next, or someone else's. We need to end this before they scalp us all in our sleep."

"You're wrong. Killing the Indians won't end this. You'll only be starting a war. Does it end when all of them are dead? When all of us are dead?" Owen yelled, but the man left the shed with no response. The sound of a tornado grew closer, and he heard the men shouting. Those twisters could tear up half the land but leave one tree standing. Unpredictable monsters, and Abbey faced them alone.

Owen scanned the tools scattered around him and saw the metal plow. If he could manage to scoot over there, perhaps he could cut himself free. He rolled until he hit a box, sat up and butt-scooted passed it, then fell on his side and rolled again. He repeated this until he managed to wedge himself between the sod wall in back and the plow. For the next several hours, he rubbed the ropes binding his hands against the plow. His arms ached, his muscles protested, but he carried on until he managed to shred some of the fibers.

Hearing the men's voices outside, he pulled on the ropes, trying to break free but he needed more time. With no other options, he rolled, twisted, shimmied and butt-scooted back to his spot.

Mr. Wallaby opened the door and stepped inside. "Thought you'd want to know that woman of yours is dead."

A surge of anger flew through him and he fought to get to his feet, to punch, hit, shoot the man for his words. "Liar. I don't believe a word you say. I know those Indians didn't attack you."

Mr. Wallaby chuckled, a menacing sound. Owen swung his legs around to trip the man, but he only hopped back another step.

"You've got plenty of fight left in you for a dead man." He squatted a few feet away, hands on his knees. "Your homestead's gone, torn through by a tornado. When the storm stopped and the moon came out, I sent my men to find your girl, but there ain't nothin' left. That fancy new house you were building is dust. Everything's demolished. No way she survived that kind of force." He sneered down at Owen then stood. "Guess you'll be seeing her again at sunrise. If you believe in that sort a thing."

"She's not dead," Owen ground out.

Mr. Wallaby pushed open the shed door. "Why you so sure? She's just a rich Southern girl who only knows how to use her charms."

A horse neighed nearby and Owen's hope rose. He could make it out of here if he could just get free. He needed to tell the town about the man's madness, and try to stop a war. "You don't know Abigail the way I do."

"No. Too bad she's dead. I would've been happy to get to know that pretty little thing better." Wallaby grabbed himself between the legs in a vulgar gesture and Owen thought he'd burn the ropes from his wrists, so much rage went through him. “Enjoy your last few hours.” Wallaby laughed loud and long into the night like a wild dog on a hunt.

Owen didn’t waste any time. He fought his way back over to the plow and rubbed twice as hard. The pain in his wrists wouldn’t stop him. The blood trickling down his hands wouldn’t stop him. Wallaby’s words wouldn’t stop him.

Wallaby had tried to break his will, but he managed to stay focused. It wouldn’t happen again. He wouldn’t believe he failed. Because if he did, that would mean Abigail really was dead.

Warmth caressed Abigail's cheek and her eyes fluttered open. Morning rays lit the sky. She blinked through the fog in her brain until she could process her surroundings. She pushed to sit up, but mind-numbing pain exploded in her right shoulder. She cried out and fisted her hands, willing herself to move. When she looked, she found a piece of wooden plank impaled into her shoulder. She gasped and cried out.

Horse hooves and wagon wheels sounded nearby. "Help," she tried, only managing a little over a whisper. "Please help me."

Owen. Was it him coming back to find her? No. He'd been taken by Mr. Wallaby and his men.

She closed her mouth and kept to the ground, waiting to see if it was friends, or enemies coming to finish what they'd started.

"Owen? Abigail?" Susan's voice rang like an angel's song.

"Here. I'm here." Abigail managed to push herself up to her knees, but they didn't see her. They pulled to a stop outside the dugout. Her throat raw and dry, she couldn't yell. The muddy ground slick from rain clung to her skirts as if entrapping her in the goo. She fought and pushed herself up onto her knees, the pain searing down her back and arm.

"Look, there." Martin pointed at Abigail.

Susan hiked up her skirts and raced through the twisted prairie grass, collapsing onto her knees in the muck beside Abigail. "Oh, you poor dear. Don't move."

"Get it out," Abigail pleaded in a hoarse tone.

Martin touched her shoulder and eyed the wood. "I don't know how deep it goes."

Abigail had seen enough shrapnel injuries from the war to know she'd already be dead if it had gone too deep. The longer they left it in there, the worse her chances of infection. Plus, she couldn't move with it still in her. "Pull it out. Trust me."

He eyed his wife and she nodded her agreement. "This is going to hurt."

"I know," Abigail managed to grind out through the discomfort. Susan took her hands and held tight as if to share her pain.

"Brace yourself," Martin warned before he yanked it free. Her insides protested as if they were ripped out along with the wood. She screamed and doubled over, the searing pain shooting down her back and arm, up her neck and deep into her chest. She heaved and panted through the worst of it until she could open her eyes once more. Through blurred vision from pain and tears, she eyed the path the men had taken. "We need to go."

"Yes, we'll get you to the doctor. Do you know where Owen is?" Susan asked.

Abigail nodded, realizing they both thought the twister had been the only enemy last night. "Wallaby got him."

"What?" Martin tossed the wood shard on the ground and took her around the waist to help her stand.

They managed to dislodge her from the muck and helped her hobble over to their wagon in front of the dugout. It was gone, all of it. No more house. No more dugout. No more barn. No more shed. Nothing was left to bring her sisters home to. Tears pricked at the corner of her eyes, but she stilled her emotions and focused on Owen. "They showed up last night, looking for an Indian. Wallaby claimed the Indian had attacked his homestead and threatened his wife, but the Indians said they didn't do it."

"How do you know that?" Susan asked, one eyebrow raising high on her forehead.

"Because we were hiding an injured Indian and his son. Trust me. They didn't do it. Owen knew that, too. We almost had them heading back to their people when Wallaby and his men showed up. If we hadn't wasted time quarreling, then we might have gotten them out of there quicker."

"Quarreling with who?" Susan asked.

"Owen. We were arguing over the fact he tried to steal my land from me."

Martin shook his head. "No, he was trying to make sure you could keep your land. I told him to tell you."

Susan shot a sideways glance at her husband. "What's going on?"

A hint of hope and fear seeped into Abigail's conscience. "I found a paper in Owen's pocket that said what the law was. I assumed he was using those laws to take my land from me, so I got mad and yelled at him." Abigail held her injured arm tight to her chest, the pain throbbing more intensely now.

"That paper came from the claims office. Owen asked Mr. Graham to inquire with Mr. Johnson of the claims office on his behalf. He was hoping the law would state that you could keep your land under the new Homestead Act, even if you aren't married. But the act only covers married women. He was trying to find a loop hole in the law so you could stay."

Abigail shook her head. Shame filled her, from mind to heart to soul. "I didn't know. Are you sure?"

"Yes, positive. That man planned on working both homesteads to make you happy. Heck, he would've given you his own home."

Her chest ached as if her heart would explode with remorse. "How could I have been so wrong? I should've listened to him."

Susan rubbed up and down her uninjured arm. "You had reason to doubt him. He wanted you to leave from the first moment you arrived. Of course, then he figured out how fabulous you are and everything changed."

Abigail smiled weakly. "We have to go now. That man is insane. He'll do anything to make the town believe he was attacked and that Owen helped a savage escape. I fear they'll do something drastic."

Martin helped her up into the back of the buckboard. "We'll ride into town and get help."

"There isn't time. They said something about him paying for his crimes at sunrise. It's sunrise now," Abigail said, she could hear the terror in her own voice, felt it in her heart.

Martin scanned the debris, his gaze settling on his wife. "You two go into town. Get her to the doctor and send help. I'll make my way to Wallaby's homestead and stall things."

"You're not going alone," Susan said.

Abigail hopped down from the wagon, attempting to hide her discomfort. "She's right."

Susan sighed, her shoulders lowered.

"You two get help," Abigail said. "I know I can stall them with false information about the Indians. Trust me. I can get in there. They were looking for me."

"It's too risky. I can't let you do this," Martin argued.

Abigail took in a long breath. "It's my fault he was caught. I shouldn't have argued with him. And he can't die thinking I hate him. Please. I have to do this."

"Owen would never forgive me if something happened to you. He'd rather die than let you risk your life for him."

Abigail spotted the rifle near the remains of the dugout. "Trust me. I don't plan on dying. We're wasting time. I'm leaving and don't try to stop me."

He held up his hands and looked at his wife who closed her eyes as if praying.

"Go with her," Susan said. "I'll get help." She kissed her husband and hopped aboard the wagon. "You both be smart. I'm not losing everyone I know on the prairie today." She snapped the reins and shot off toward town.

Abigail retrieved the rifle and began walking toward Wallaby's place, but she knew they'd never make it in time. Not on foot. Still, she had to try.

About three hundred yards from their pasture, she spotted a horse, the one Owen had saddled for the Indian last night. The Indian had either been caught or he sent it back. She hoped it was the latter. She could only handle saving one life at a time, and Owen was her first priority.

She and Martin mounted the horse and galloped across the open fields until they reached the edge of

Wallaby's land. Her head dizzy with pain, she fought not to swoon and fall from the horse with each stride. "Stop. We need to stop."

Martin pulled the reins back and she slid from the horse, fighting the darkness that threatened to take her.

"You can barely stand up. There's no way you can fight them like this.

"I don't plan to fight them. There are too many of them. Like you said, I need to stall them." Abigail pointed to some trees and rocks nearby. "Stay there unless you hear me screaming then run."

He gripped her wrist. "No. I'm coming with you."

Abigail nodded. "Yes, but not yet. We need to stall them if we can, so I'll go first. I'll get them to listen to me. Then you'll do what you did earlier, ride in on this horse to check on everyone after the storm."

Martin nodded. "Fine, but ten minutes head start is all you get."

"Twenty, and not a minute sooner." She passed the reins to him and hobbled across the field toward the Wallaby's place.

Men were standing out front of his home, chatting when she managed to get close enough to yell.

"Help. Please, help me!" She didn't have to pretend to be weak and wounded this time, or that she'd pass out. Men came running, some with guns drawn. "It's that girl. Abigail McKinnie."

"Get her!" Wallaby shouted from the doorway of his home.

They dragged her to him and dropped her on her knees. "You've got some gumption, girl. What happened to you?"

She let the tears fall, the ones she'd held in when her brothers were killed, her sister was attacked, her crops were burned, her house destroyed. They came freely for the first time and she sobbed, only managing a few words. "Indians. Hurt. You. Were. Right."

He stomped his foot. "You hear that, men? The girl got what she deserved for helping those savages." He ripped her dress in the back where the wood had punctured her skin. "See what those savages do to women and children. Are we going to continue to allow this?"

"No!" two men shouted.

She scanned the area, looking for Owen, but she couldn't find him. *Dear Lord, don't let him be hurt or killed.*

Wallaby squatted in front of her. "Don't worry. We'll take care of them savages, and I'll take care of you, too," he said in a suggestive tone.

Her stomach roiled with the thought of this man touching her, but certainly he wouldn't dare. His wife wouldn't let him. He wouldn't harm her in front of all these witnesses.

"Don't look so sad." He touched her face, sending chills down her skin. His breath smelled of stale tobacco and rotting meat, making her stomach roll. "Mary, get out here! You need to doctor this girl while we go hang ourselves a traitor and shoot some savages."

The woman she had seen at church came outside and looked down at Abigail. "Woman needs a doctor. That's a deep wound."

"You'll manage." He scowled down at Mary. A baby cried inside and she eyed the doorway before she nodded her agreement.

"Wait. No. Owen didn't hurt anyone. It was me. He was only protecting me. I thought I could tame the savages, but I was wrong. I should be the one punished."

Wallaby leaned down and whispered in her ear, "I'll punish you later in my own way." Then he straightened and turned to his men. "You two, get her inside then grab Baker. If she gives you any trouble tie her down until we're done."

Abigail shoved away from Mary and scratched Wallaby's face from eye to chin. He back-handed her, sending her to the ground. A hot sting radiated over her cheek. Face in the dirt, she looked up to see a gun pointed at her mouth and Wallaby's eyes shining with the light of death.

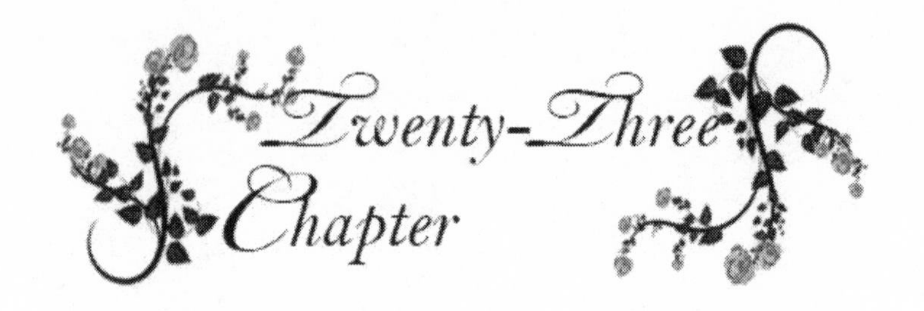

Chapter Twenty-Three

A commotion outside the shed drove Owen to work quickly on the rope around his legs. The sunlight streaming through the cracks around the door told him it was already sunrise.

Men shouted then a woman screamed and he froze.

Abigail?

The ties around his wrists finally gave way and he pulled them off. Blood oozed from the burns, but he couldn't feel the pain. His pulse thundered in his ears and he made quick work of the rope binding his feet.

Another woman yelled and he heard a scuffle outside. He raced to the door and peered through the cracks. There was Abigail, a gun only inches from her delicate face. He had to do something.

Before he could try to shove the shed door open, one of the men stepped toward Abigail. "You can't just shoot her. I thought we were protecting our lands and our wives and our children."

"No. All my husband wants to do is win. He always has to win," Mary said with venom in her voice. "And Mr. Baker made him look like a fool in church so he—"

Wallaby spun, hitting his wife with the side of his gun. She cried out and grabbed her cheek.

Owen made use of the distraction, shoved the door open and raced for the men. If he could tackle one of them, he could get the man's gun and give Abigail a chance to escape.

A shot was fired before he could reach them. He halted and sucked in a quick breath, but saw that Abigail was okay. He looked further into the distance and spotted Martin with a rifle pointed at the sky.

"You're surrounded, Wallaby. The town wants you to come in to answer some questions."

Owen rushed to Lenard's side and grabbed the gun from his hand. The majority of the men had their hands raised in the air in surrender.

"We don't want no trouble. Just wanted to protect our land is all," Lenard said.

Wallaby grabbed Abigail, pulling her in front of him to use her as a human shield. "You're all so stupid. They're gonna kill us all if we don't kill them first. I know. They slaughtered my first wife and sleeping baby while I was off hunting. They'll do it again. Their savages. They're nothing but blood-thirsty monsters." His hands shook and Owen feared the gun would go off even if he didn't mean to shoot.

Some of the men joined Wallaby in a standoff against Owen and Martin.

"The townspeople need to know we're looking out for them. It's time to take our land we work and make sure they can't ruin it again. And I ain't gonna take a chance with my wife and young'un." Wallaby tightened his grip around Abigail's throat, and her face turned a deep red. "Where are these townspeople you've got? I don't see no one but you."

Mary rose from the ground and kicked dirt at Wallaby. "You've never let them go. I've never meant nothin' to you but to be a replacement for your first wife."

Owen tilted his head toward Martin, gesturing for his friend to move closer while Wallaby was distracted but two other men caught sight of his movement and pointed a gun at him.

Owen covered him, but knew if this ended up in a gun battle Abigail would lose. He needed to get her away from Wallaby. Martin side-stepped around the men to join Owen near Abigail.

She bucked and squirmed and gave Wallaby a fight, but she couldn't break free. He saw blood on the side of her dress, the fabric torn at the shoulder. What had he done to her? Owen stepped forward, but Martin grabbed his shirt and pulled him back. "It won't be long before Susan gets people from town here. Just need to stall. Keep him talking."

Martin aimed the rifle at one of the men, but Owen lowered his weapon to his side and inched forward. "I know what you're talking about. Losing a wife, people you love. I've lost many. Brothers, my mother, father, sister, and my own wife, and a child. He wasn't mine by blood, but when I lowered his limp body into the ground, I felt the loss all the same. I thought that keeping myself away from others would keep me from feeling that pain again, but all it did was make me unhappy. It wasn't until I let the pain and fear go that I started living again."

Wallaby shifted Abigail and drove the gun into her temple. "That's far enough."

Owen stopped his advance. "You can't conquer your fears with a gun."

"I ain't afraid!" Wallaby shouted at him, but Owen saw it in his eyes. Fear was the only thing this man had left to cling to in life.

"You can't control life, or danger. You can only try to live the best you can. Killing innocent people isn't the answer."

"Innocent? I told you those savages burned the mill and then came here."

"I'm not talking about the Indians. You have a woman in your arms with a gun to her head. How did you get here?" Owen dared another step, but Wallaby tightened his hold on Abigail, the color of her face turning a darker shade of red. If Owen didn't do something soon, Wallaby would choke her to death.

"You still claim she's innocent? I'll tell you what. I'll let her go if you surrender. Admit you helped that savage and you deserve to hang for it, and I'll let her go."

Abigail swung her head back, popping him in the nose. He released her instantly. Blood gushed down his face onto his shirt. She gasped and choked. Crying out in anger, Wallaby smacked her in the face. Owen raced forward. Shots rang out, followed by shouts and cries.

All breath was knocked from his lungs.

More shots sounded and he doubled over. Out of the corner of his eye, he saw Abigail break free and grab a gun. More shots then flames licked his insides, searing his chest. His knees hit the ground. His lungs spasmed, trying to take in air, but no breaths entered.

His mind faded until only one thought remained… Abigail.

Abigail's hands shook and the world blurred. She dropped the gun and scooted away. People scattered around them. A man hovered over her.

"Shot him?" She heard her own voice as if someone else spoke, distant and faint.

Hands touched her shoulder and the world began to settle. Her pulse still pounded, her breath still held tight in her lungs, but she managed to hear again, to focus.

"He had it coming," Mary said from behind.

"You shut up, woman," Wallaby bit out.

That was when Abigail noticed Mary had got him in the leg. Two men restrained him and began pulling him toward other men with rifles. He fought and kicked with his good leg but all it did was cause him to yelp in pain from the gunshot wound.

Then she saw Owen on the ground, blood saturating his shirt. She clawed to stand, but someone had her, their hands on her shoulders. She looked up to find Martin.

"You need the doctor. Stay still. That wound's opened up more."

She turned in his arms. "Please. I need to get to Owen. I have to tell him…" She broke before she could finish her words, but Martin seemed to understand. With one arm under her legs and the other at her back, he lifted her and carried her. The tiny jolt and pressure on her back caused dizzying pain, but she managed to stay conscious even when he lowered her to the ground next to Owen.

The smell of blood and gunpowder filled her with terror. She grabbed his hand and held it to her chest. "Owen, I'm so sorry. I was wrong. I was terribly wrong."

His eye lids fluttered, but she didn't know if he could hear her. "Please, Owen. Don't die on me. Doctor! Where's the doctor?"

A man she didn't recognize rushed over, but he angled to check her wound instead. "No. Him first."

Stunned, the man nodded then went to work on Owen. "I need to stop the bleeding. Help me lift him." They sat Owen up and he cried out like a wounded calf. His eyes rolled back in his head.

Abigail kept hold of his hand, willing him to fight.

"Looks like the bullet didn't go all the way through. I need to operate. Bring a table outside so I can see in the light."

Abigail's body trembled at his words. She felt cold, despite the warm late-summer sun.

"Clean the wound," the doctor was saying. "I'll be over to operate in a minute. Get some horse blankets and anything else you can find, and get her inside. She's in shock. Wrap her up and keep her warm. Build a fire if you must. I'll be in to stitch her up shortly after I'm done with this man and the one over there. And two others."

Martin slipped his arms under her shoulders to lift her, but she wouldn't let go of Owen's hand. "No, I won't leave him. I can't."

Susan appeared beside her and stroked her cheeks. "If you want him to live, you must let the doctor do what he can. You heard him. If the bullet didn't hit anything major, he'll be fine." She pried Abigail's shaking fingers from Owen's. "That's it." Then Martin lifted her once more and carried her into Wallaby's soddie.

Abigail's joints ached from the shaking, her head ached from a lump she must've gotten during the twister, and her shoulder throbbed from the puncture wound. By the time she stopped shaking and the doctor entered, she could barely keep her eyes open from exhaustion. "Is he…"

"He's resting on the table the men pulled outside. I managed to remove the bullet and a small bone fragment from his rib. It looks good so far. The next twenty-four hours are critical. We'll need to move him inside for the night and see how things go. The men are setting up some tents outside. I'll be staying until all the men are stable.

Abigail fought to respond, her mind fading fast. "Thank you, doctor."

He dropped his bag on the floor by the chair and knelt. "Don't thank me yet. You're not going to like this next part. I need to check your wound and remove the remaining bits of wood I saw, not to mention any others in that wound. Then I need to stitch you up."

Susan knelt in front of the chair and held her hands. "I'll stay with you, Abigail. And don't worry about Owen. He's strong."

Abigail nodded and held tight to Susan. The first splinter slid out without any real pain.

"Now I have to dig a little deeper. Feel free to scream all you want."

Abigail took a deep breath. It felt like he was using a butcher knife to cut through the muscle in her back. The intense pressure and sharp pain made her eyes water. She grinded her teeth, but couldn't find the strength to cry out.

"You're doing great," the doctor said encouragingly. "What happened?"

Martin answered for her. "The twister. I found her in a ditch covered in mud, a piece of wood was lodged in her shoulder. I pulled it out the best I could."

"You did great." The doctor went deeper and Abigail started to fade, her body shutting down. Then she swooned. She fought not to faint, to give into the darkness, but darkness won.

When Abigail woke up, it was dark and quiet. She shot up and then cried out in pain. Susan raced to her side. "Here. Drink some water."

Abigail welcomed the coolness on her raw, dry throat. When she had her fill, she took a deep breath and asked, "Where's Owen? I want to see Owen."

"He's doing okay. He woke up a little bit ago, too, but he's resting now."

Abigail wanted to go to him, but before she even sat up, darkness took her once more.

It wasn't until the next day when sunlight poured in through the front window that she awoke and felt well enough to rise from her bed. "Please. Take me to him."

Susan helped her from the bed. They reached the door and saw men mounting horses and racing away. "Where're they going?"

Susan bowed her head and held tight to Abigail's good arm, helping her walk. "I'm afraid they're still convinced that the Indians will attack. Someone spotted them near your land and they went into town to form a posse to drive them off."

"People will get killed." Abigail shook her head. "I wish they'd stop being so scared and wanting to fight all the time. I'm tired of fighting."

The first autumn breeze blew through the prairie and she knew they wouldn't last the winter without a proper home. She spotted Owen propped up near a fire with men around him, Preacher Elijah at his side. Her breath caught at the sight, worried the preacher was reading Owen's last rights.

"Calm down. You're all tense again. He's just visiting with Owen. They're talking about what happened and about the Indians."

Abigail managed to reach Owen who looked up with a slack jaw and raised brows. He didn't know.

"You don't remember me telling you before you passed out, do you?"

"Telling me what?" Owen asked.

Susan helped her lower to the ground then she, Preacher Elijah, and everyone else scattered to give her and Owen privacy. "About the fact that I'm not worthy of you."

His lips spread wide, matching his eyes. "You believe me now?"

She nodded. "Owen. I was so stupid. I've been promised things before. That men would help us save our way of life. Men would protect us when the Union soldiers came. Men would help us survive after the soldiers left us in ruins. No one ever kept their promises. I thought…I thought you only wanted my land."

"Abbey." He lifted his arm, but winced in pain. She snuggled closer to him, careful not to lean her bad shoulder against the ground, knowing she still couldn't manage any pressure against her skin. His fingers brushed her lips then caressed her face. "All I want is you."

Her heart floated to Heaven at his words. "You don't hate me for not believing you?"

"I could never hate you. We've both suffered greatly in our lives, but I think it's time we started trusting each other." He rested his forehead to hers. "Do you think you can do that? Trust me?"

"Yes," she whispered. "You won't want my land now anyway."

"Why?" he asked, his lips edging toward hers.

"It was destroyed by that twister the other day. There's nothing left, Owen. We won't survive the winter." A rise of fear that she'd not only let her sisters down, but now she'd have to leave her land, too, made her heart sting more than her wound.

"We'll figure it out together." He pressed his lips lightly to hers, not caring who watched. The contact sent her pulse fluttering and her heart flipping with want and need to be with this man forever.

When their lips parted, she felt she'd given part of herself to him forever. Hope emerged through the ashes of sorrow and for the first time, she believed in happiness.

"We need to go."

Abigail sat back, her hand moving to his forehead to check for fever. "Go where?"

"To our homestead." Owen managed to sit up and wave Elijah over to them.

She held him down, not wanting him to reopen his wound. "I told you there's nothing left."

He took her hand and kissed her fingers. “If I have you, I have everything.”

Abigail was right. As far as the buildings, equipment, and animals were concerned, there was nothing left. Owen fought the self-pity and despair at all their hard work wasted. After one glance at Abigail crawling out of the back of the wagon with him, he knew none of those things mattered. "We'll figure it out. I promise."

Horses galloped toward them just as Owen had feared. The posse had assembled quickly and headed onto his land, only there were no Indians to murder. Preacher Elijah, Susan, and Martin joined them at the edge of the demolished dugout. "What can we do for you?" Owen asked, keeping Abigail close to his side.

"Came to protect you from savages. Heard they were here," Lenard said, his voice sounding strained as if he'd rather be elsewhere. No doubt he was trying to save face in front of the men.

Elijah stepped forward. “As you can see, there is nothing left here to protect.”

The sheriff straightened his hat. “Sorry to see this. It’s tough ’round these parts.” He looked straight at Abigail. “Might want to consider heading back home.”

Owen moved forward, but Abigail kept hold of him. “I think we’ll be fine, but thank you for your concern.”

The group started to turn their horses back toward town when one of the men pointed. “What’s that up on the hill?” They all turned to see something white sticking up from the ground.

Before Owen could stop them, Lenard yelled, “Let’s go!” They tore off over the field toward the hill. Elijah, Susan, Martin, Owen and Abigail followed as quickly as they could, making their way to the tall tree on the hill near the creek.

Susan held tight to her husband who eyed Owen as they walked. “Doc says you were lucky that bullet didn’t do more damage, but you still need to take it easy.”

“I can’t let them kill for no reason.” When they finally reached the top of the hill where the men stood, they found a white tepee with a fire pit in front of it.

"They can't settle on your land," Lenard said. "Now you ready to take care of those Injuns?"

Owen eyed the structure then peered inside and he found his hat, trench coat, and horse blanket. The warmth of the gesture took his breath away. "They're not moving onto our land. They built us a home since ours was destroyed."

Elijah smiled. "Doesn't sound like savages to me. Sounds like good neighbors."

Lenard lowered his hat to his chest and shook his head. "Well, I'll be. Never saw nothin' like this before."

Abigail cleared her throat. "I think the real savage is already in the sheriff's custody. The man who kidnapped Owen and tried to murder him, not to mention abusing his wife and threatening me. A man who lied about Indians attacking his property and threatening his family."

"He's still claiming that's true," the sheriff said.

"Have you ever seen a true Indian attack that only burned a board or two, or heard of them threatening someone without following through on it?" Owen asked. "These are not those kind of Indians. They're peaceful. They want the same thing we want, to build a life here on the prairie.

Besides, Wallaby admitted to me that he burned his own property just to stir up more hatred. Many of the men heard his rantings. He lost his first wife and family to an Indian attack and wanted revenge. These Indians aren't the ones who attacked him. And we should leave them in peace."

"Still don't make it right that they burned our mill. Men were hurt." The sheriff straightened his belt and eyed the terrain across the creek.

Owen nodded his agreement. "Yes, but from what I understand this used to be their land, before the white men drove them off it and claimed it as their own. It's got to be hard to let that go. That's only if the fire was truly set by them. I have my doubts now that Mr. Wallaby's true character has become apparent."

The sheriff planted his hat on his head and mounted his horse. "Come on, men. It's time we focus on getting ready for winter instead of wasting our time looking for trouble that ain't there." He turned his horse to head back, but paused. "If they pick another fight, though, we'll be the ones to make sure there are none of them left to make trouble in the future."

Owen relaxed into Abigail and they watched the men gallop away. “Do you think they’ll keep their word and leave the Indians alone?”

“We can hope,” Abigail said.

Owen eyed the tepee, his friends, Preacher Elijah and then turned to Abbey, taking her hands in his. “I want to give you everything you’ve ever dreamed of. I want to be the man that keeps every promise to you. If I could, I’d build you a real home today. I’d shower you with gifts, have all your sisters here by your side, but I can’t. I know I have very little to offer, but I promise to try to make you the happiest woman on the prairie. I believe anything is possible while you’re by my side. We’ll rebuild, and we’ll get your sisters here as quick as we can. Are you still willing to marry me?”

She pulled her hand away and his heart sank, only to soar to the heavens as she caressed his face. “Yes.”

“I know it’s sudden, but I can’t wait much longer. I want you to be my wife today, now. We have the preacher and our friends here, but no fancy gown or church. Only my offer to love you always. If you’ll have me, we’ll be partners in everything.”

“I don’t need fancy. I just need you,” she said, her eyes filling with tears.

He took her in his arms and kissed her with all the passion he'd held inside for so long. Here, in this rough and wild land, they would build a home, grow crops and make a family. They would still struggle with hard times, but they would have each other. For the rest of their days, they would remain partners, loving each other on the prairie.

The End

Acknowledgements

I'd like to thank Cissie Patterson and Dara Schroader for taking the time to beta read this story. Also, I'd like to thank my street team for all their support, and Amber Garcia for being the best virtual assistant an author could dream of working with.

DEAR READER,

I hope you've enjoyed the first installment of the McKinnie Mail Order Brides series. This series has been a pleasure to research and write over these last several months. It's provided me with the opportunity to consult with some of my local museums in the Kennesaw, Georgia area. My kids have even helped with some of the research since they are history buffs.

If you enjoyed the sweet tone of this book, I encourage you to try my contemporary romance series, Sweetwater County. Start with book one, Winter in Sweetwater County for the best reading experience.

Happy reading,
Ciara Knight

Other Books by Ciara Knight

For a complete list of my books, please visit my website at www.ciaraknight.com. A great way to keep up to date on all releases, sales and prizes subscribe to my newsletter at www.ciaraknight.com/newsletter. I'm extremely sociable, so feel free to chat with me on Facebook (ciaraknightwrites), Twitter (@ciaratknight) or Goodreads.

For your convenience please see my complete title list below, in reading order:

CONTEMPORARY ROMANCE

Sweetwater County Series

Winter in Sweetwater County

Spring in Sweetwater County

Fall in Sweetwater County

Christmas in Sweetwater County

Valentines in Sweetwater County

Fourth of July in Sweetwater County

Thanksgiving in Sweetwater County

Grace in Sweetwater County

Faith in Sweetwater County (coming soon)

Hope n Sweetwater County (coming soon)

Love in Sweetwater County (coming soon)

Riverbend series

Riverbend (novella)

In All My Wishes

In All My Years

In All My Dreams

In All my Life

Gone with the Brides

Sassy Bride

Sweet Bride

Southern Bride

YOUNG ADULT PARANORMAL

Battle for Souls Series

Rise From Darkness

Fall From Grace

Ascension of Evil

The Neumarian Chronicles

Weighted

Escapement

Pendulum

Balance

ADULTA HIGH FANTASY

The Shrouded Kingdoms

The Curse of Gremdon

The Secrets of Dargon

The Runes of Bramon (Coming 2018)

HISTORICAL WEATERN ROMANCE

McKinnie Mail Order Brides

Love on the Prairie

Love in the Rockies (Coming soon)

Love on the Plains (Coming soon)

A Prospectors Novel

Fools Rush

American Mail Order Brides

Adelaide: Bride of Maryland